Cities of the Absurd

Strange Tales from
the Dark Metropolis

Kenneth Francis

En Route Books and Media, LLC
Saint Louis, MO

ENROUTE
Make the time

En Route Books and Media, LLC
5705 Rhodes Avenue
St. Louis, MO 63109

Contact us at contactus@enroutebooksandmedia.com

Cover art by Sebastian Mahfood using DALL-E
Copyright 2025 Kenneth Francis

ISBN: 979-8-88870-384-7
Library of Congress Control Number: 2025940269

Table of Contents

Literary style and themes:

The genre for *Cities of the Absurd* is a fusion of Gothic Horror, Theatre of the Absurd, and Christian Theism, as well as Dark Romanticism, humour, infused with metaphor, satire, and echoes of a modern-day Poe and Kafka with a pinch of science fiction. It will hopefully appeal to the readers' taste for terrifying or psychologically stimulating them.

Due to the Lockdowns and crazy Woke policies of 2020, the world moved beyond Theatre of the Absurd into a turbo-absurd mode, thus becoming a bleak reality, and nowhere was it more present than in the cold-hearted cities of the West, particularly the nocturnal streets of America.

The Burning Mattress

I hate Tuesdays. I think it's a man thing. Most of the women I know and have met hate Mondays. The thought of treating myself to a few whiskeys at the weekend seems a thousand years away on Tuesday. At least on Mondays, I'm resigned to the long week ahead. And in the autumn of my life, I've got to hold out and be careful not to damage further my abused liver. But for now, it's a dreaded second day of the week in early spring that I must endure; though, I have to admit, sometimes the anticipation of weekend boozing is better than physically gulping it down. A bit like climbing a mountain, only to experience a tinge of anti-climax at reaching the summit as the rain begins to fall.

Meanwhile, there's still a bit of frost on the backyard lawn, and I noticed a mangey mouse on the grass scurrying towards the garden shed. I thought, what could this scruffy little rodent be thinking of, and where is it going? Maybe it lives under the shed? Or maybe it's lost? Or could it be on its way to the *Annual General Meeting of Mangey Mice Who Live Under Sheds*? Whatever the reason, I had to let my dog Geezer slip out through the sliding glass doors to do his business on the grass. From a young boy aged six, I had outlived nine dogs, and it made me sad to think that old Geezer had three paws in the pet cemetery. Despite his age, he ran around the yard, where the sparrows were having a royal banquet in the birdfeed that I erected many years ago when Geezer was a puppy. Forever living in the past, my memory is razor sharp. I remember buying Geezer as a puppy and how he was highly strung for such a little Jack Russell. The old cockney breeder said to me, "'E's a right little geezer, that fella", hence, the name I called him. But I never thought he'd live so long.

After I let him out into the yard on this chilly Tuesday morning, I noticed puffs of smoke rising behind the fence of my next-door neighbour's garden. The smell of the smoke evoked a memory from when I was a young man. It was in November on a quiet street on the edge of the city when the shades of day ebbed into twilight time; when the winter flu was blowing through homes and schools, and almost every football player looked hairy and middle-aged. It was also a time when the world seemed normal and not insane, despite being wonderfully crazy and full of adventure. Although it wasn't the Victorian era, even the modern times of yesteryear can seem quite old-fashioned when looking back.

On that particular evening in my memory, I felt a light wind on my face, as I slowly cycled down a long street of Georgian five-storey houses to a place where I was stationed to work for three weeks. The prefab office was beside these houses which have long since been destroyed by the wrecking-balls of council tsars. Those bureaucratic bums were nothing short of architectural vandals who knelt at the altar of Brutalism. They had delusions of intellectual grandeur and were quite patronising to their more intelligent female assistants. They usually supported the Labour Party and drove 'Mark 2' Jaguar cars or Bentley T-series. The few nice ones, who were genuinely bright, kept their heads down but never got promoted. The key Omerta rules for promotion back then were: Always 'zip your trap' and 'never rat on senior fellow councillors'.

To my shame, I, too, had a brief stint working for the tsars who wanted rid of those beautiful Georgian wonders. I got the job to take part in this destruction because my late father, who was a porter in the housing department, "put in a word for me". You could call it nepotism in low places. I also lied on my resume, saying I had vast experience in supervision and mediation. In fact, I was a bragger and full of intellectual pride; a talentless, low-grade civil servant, although I told my friends I was a senior official who worked in a plush office and supervised a team of 15 staff. I even said that I was extremely popular with the pretty female staff, despite being 'invisible'.

In reality, my office was a small prefab, frequented by heavy-smoking middle-aged, inside a depot called 'The Yard'. During summer months, the prefab stunk of stale nicotine and there was always the odd bin truck parked outside. Once a week, my supervisor would pay me a visit to see how things were going with the slaughter of the Georgian strip. He was an elderly man with a large head who married a younger woman, and they had one teenage boy. I used to dread seeing the supervisor walk up to the prefab every Thursday afternoon, as he never had a nice word to say to me, often criticising me for filling out the forms the wrong way. He seemed obsessed with forms.

On the week my contract was finalised, with four days left to work, I waited nervously in the office for him to arrive. I was feeling agitated because I accidently broke an electric two-bar heater by spilling tea all over it. But instead of my manager arriving at the prefab, a young teenage boy dressed in a school uniform walked up and knocked on the door. He told me that he was the manager's son, and when he entered the office, he looked quite sad. He said his dad died 'last night' after collapsing on the floor with a brain aneurism and he was here, in his place, to collect the forms. The bad side of my brain made me feel all my birthdays had come at once, while the good side of my soul descended into a maelstrom of guilt and shame. Talk about mixed emotions. It was like winning the lottery and being run over by a bus at the same time. I tried to comfort him with the usual cliché platitudes of 'he's at peace now', but he just nodded his head and smiled. He told me his father's last words were, 'Don't forget the forms'.

As soon as the boy left the yard, I also locked up the prefab and headed to visit the tenants in the Georgian strip's east side. Wearing a Trilby hat,

Macintosh coat, I carried a leather satchel as I cycled along the road. One of the Georgian tenants said I looked like 'Inspector Clouseau' from the *Pink Panther* movies. I initially regarded the blue-collared tenants as inferior. But to my surprise, some of them made the Queen sound common. I often wondered, how did they end up financially broke in such an impoverished slum, despite the buildings' faded grandeur? What could it have been that caused such a fall from a former status of class to life at the bottom? Drink? Family breakup? Sexual abuse? Perhaps I'll never know. All I knew at the time was it was my job to persuade the Georgian folk to relocate beyond the city, where satellite towns were springing up rapidly around the wastelands of suburbia.

I knocked on many doors and handed the tenants forms to fill in if they wanted to move out. At one door, a little attractive widow seemed to flirt with me, but I resisted her smiles out of respect for my then girlfriend, who subsequently left me a year later because I didn't make her happy. The widow didn't look too happy either. Aged in her late 30s, she invited me in for tea, to a flat that smelt of stale cigarette. The shag carpet looked like a cement truck tipped a tonne of macaroni onto the floor and it later dried up, while the curtains looked like Liberace's bath robes. Like most 1970s furnishing, it was a time that taste forgot: Japanese maple-flower-patterned wallpaper adorned the walls; in the kitchen, I could see a lemon-coloured Formica table, with a speckled pattern that looked like hundreds of squashed ants. The silk dressing gowan she wore was the garish 'leopard-skin' type. She told me she never married, but her deceased boyfriend lived with her for eight years before dying of pneumonia.

Standing across the room from me, she took a record out of its sleeve and placed it on the turnstile of a mahogany radio record player. As she strolled back to the table and sat down, the song came on player, a chart hit by Hurricane Smith called, "Oh Babe What Would You Say." A little Yorkshire terrier jumped onto her lap, and he growled lowly every time I spoke. She said, "The mothers round here are stuck-up witches. The men are okay, but their wives are no friends of mine." I nodded in faux empathy at her moaning and spoofed her by saying I read lots of astrologer books and had visionary skills. To her amazement, I told her lots of things about her life which, unbeknownst to her, I saw referenced on her tenant profile. I even told her, her mother's maiden name (that, too, was on her profile). I told her these things, as I blew a smoke ring from my big, phallic cigar, unaware of the vulvic undertones of the spinning vapour ring that hovered between us. I must've looked like a right pathetic jerk trying to appear cool and prophetic during that Freudian moment, despite nervously sipping my tea before leaving her with a bunch of forms as thick as a telephone directory.

I couldn't wait to exit the room, as I knew her dog hated me, and her leg-crossing was revealing more flesh by the minute. But I didn't leave the building. I did a quick B-line to the floor below her, where lived an intellectually impaired family who wouldn't invite me in but stood at the door perplexed at the vast paper-work I encouraged them to fill out. There was a foul stench of unwashed feet and boiled cabbage wafting about from their flat as I stood there. I subsequently heard from a co-worker some weeks later that the mother in the family had a stroke and subsequently lay dead in bed for six days on the day I arrived. Her husband was an alcoholic who was in prison serving time for the manslaughter of another drunk who mocked his pregnant, unmarried daughter. And when his children visited him in jail, the first thing he would ask them was, "Is Rex okay? Does he miss me?" (Rex was their pet Staffordshire bull terrier.) Meanwhile, the siblings kept leaving their dead mother food by her bedside, while the obese Rex would secretly creep into the room and eat it until the visiting social worker arrived one day to discover the corpse.

Those young social workers had to deal with worse cases than this. Some of the females were quite attractive. They wore flairs and 'hotpants' and would get together at dance halls every weekend. They looked much older than their chronicle age, smoked Rothmans' cigarettes and ate fish-and-chips every Friday. During summer week-days on the tenement Georgian strip, the smell of bacon and cabbage emanated from the hallways. Some days, the sight of a pack of panting dogs running quickly down the street was quite common. The summertime Number One pop song earlier that year, audible from one of the house's half-open windows, was a politically incorrect cracker that encouraged young men with women on their minds, to *'have a drink, have a drive, go out and see what you can find'.*

But during that November, there was no music playing and I remember looking up at the windows and seeing 50-watt bulbs without shades hanging from the ceilings, as I passed by each evening on my way home from work. I could also see flickering shadows on the rooms' gaudy, geometric floral wallpaper and hear the sound of a baby bawling. Some of the tenants were so poor they had broadsheet newspapers hanging on their windows instead of curtains. But that didn't take away from the beauty of the decaying, Georgian architecture. Paradoxically, the discontentment of the tenants there was not as bad as the misery of the inhabitants of leafy suburbia, where things were meant to be better but were in fact worse because they were meant to be better. I bet even the ghosts who once spooked the vacant Georgian buildings, long after the tenants had presumably died, must have gone away for good; for what is there to haunt in two giant car-park blocks, locked-down in silence in the dead of night?

In the adjoining tenement building, I knocked on a door on the first floor. A tall elderly man in a dark suit came behind me with a key in his hand while he opened the door and entered the flat. He slowly turned around, but didn't look me in the eye, keeping his head down. He had a hump-back and appeared to be extremely shy. When I told him who I was, he shouted into the room, 'Haninooa!' I wondered if he was calling his mother, father, brother, sister, or lover. Or perhaps his pet cat or dog. What kind of name is 'Haninooa'? It turned out to be his brother: A lanky older man wearing a dressing gowan. There was something of the Victorian undertaker about the pair of them. He invited me into the flat and told his brother to go back into his room. We drank some tea, and he gave me a Mars Bar. Although I didn't want it, I took it out of politeness but didn't eat it. He told me he lived with his brother for the past 40 years and said the flat hasn't changed in all that time.

The room was dark and full of Victorian furniture. There was a coal fire lighting, and on the mantlepiece were dozens of long thinly cut pieces of newspaper, each one the size of a pencil. The man put another cigarette in his mouth and reached down to the fire with one of the paper strips, thus lighting his cigarette. He sat down and began telling me things about the house that I already knew. As he spoke, he started doodling on the paper table covering with a razor-sharp 4H pencil. The table-cloth was covered with numerous abstract doodles. Some of the doodles looked like flabby balloons, while others resembled untrimmed hedgerows. He told me of how 'handy' it was doodling with a 4H pencil as he didn't have to sharpen it too often, and he went into great detail about how the inferior 4B pencils' lead nibs keep breaking when being sharpened with a pairer, despite them giving a darker effect to the doodles. His exotic knowledge on the merits and drawbacks of different graded pencil leads was both impressive and mind-numbingly excruciating. He also spoke at great length about how many strips of paper he gets out of one page of newspaper to light his cigarettes with, saying the broadsheets yield more strips because of their bigger size and are better value for money.

I tried to interrupt him to de-rail from such extremely boring topics, but he soon returned to them after a minute or two, telling me about every single item he buys in the supermarket and how prices have risen compared to the previous year. Then, alas! he spoke about the tenants living in the building: 'The flats are divided up into 10, two of each facing one another,' he said. 'Below me live two old spinsters who no sane man would marry, and beside them a crazy, bearded woman with cats; her name's Lizzie and she shouts a lot at night and this frightens Eddie: that's my brother who you've just met. But worst of all is the small man in the basement: A gas-meter inspector who owns a vicious Dalmatian with one eye, who tried to have sex with my leg and regularly shits the hallway.' 'What happened to his eye?' I asked. 'He got into a scrap with one of Lizzie's cats. Dogs always come out the worst when scrapping with cats. He's such a pest. Actually, while you're here, I want to make an official complaint on the dog and have him removed from the house. Can you do that?' I asked him why he didn't confront his neighbour years ago about this, and he told me that was the council's job, not his. He also said the same about a broken hinge on his front door that was hanging loose for over 12 years. I told

him I'd take a note of the dog and try to have the
RSPCA remove the animal.

No sooner had I said that, the mad bearded
woman in the basement started shouting, "*You won't
throw sheep's heads outside my door at three o'clock
in the morning!*' The scream must've triggered Eddie,
who was in the toilet, and he responded by
chanting, '*Aa'na, hen'en'ua, a'na, hen'en'ua, henenu
henenu henenua…!*' I asked his brother was he
practising some kind of yoga or Native American
Indian war dance. He laughed and told me the words
are a mystery, but they might refer to a girl he once
met many years ago at a hen party; her name was
Anna. He said Eddie sometimes still pines for her and
he gets frustrated, but he'd be far too shy and
'retarded' now to ask any woman out on a date. The
brother also told me that Eddie is like a big child, but
he can manage to do house chores and cycle his bike.
'The social workers advised me to send him to an
asylum to live, but I wouldn't do it. He comes in
handy for shopping and cleaning the house, and his
disability welfare cheque helps pay the rent. He can
even ride his bike while carrying a bag of coal. He
only gets confused when he sometimes starts

chanting the wrong words, like "hang-an-a, hang-an-a, din-in-uh-in-in-uh-in-in-in-a", but I quickly correct him when he panics by shouting back at him, "It's, Hen'en'ua,a'na, hen'en'ua!" That seems to calm him down and he continues with the right words. I actually get great pleasure out of correcting him; would you like to correct him if he gets confused again? I can write down the words for you.' he asked me. 'I'd love to see how he reacts to a strange voice, especially if you knock him off track by shouting, "It's Na-na-na-na, ba gama-ga-ma", not "din-in-uh-ah".'

At this point, I didn't know whether to laugh or commit hari-kari with his 4H pencil. I would've even accepted spontaneous human combustion as a quick and painless death. And when Eddie started to chant again, the dog downstairs started to bark and the crazy woman squealed, *"Am'in I right? am'in I right?"* My head began to spin, and I told his brother I'd be back another day to help him fill out the form. But as I was leaving the building, the Dalmatian was standing at the hall door panting and drooling beside a big, steaming turd. I could sense he had leg-rape on his mind, and I froze with my back against the wall when he started to growl at me. The building and street were quiet, but I could hear the sound of a jackhammer pounding pavement in the distance. I remembered the half-eaten Mars Bar that I had in my pocket, so I slowly took it out and threw it at the dog. As he started chewing the bar, I walked out of the building and headed towards my bicycle which I had chained to a lamppost across the road.

It was late afternoon and getting dark and a large queue of nurses had gathered at a bus stop on their way to work their night shift. I knew they were nurses because some of them were wearing their scrubs. Suddenly, I heard the sound of boys laughing emanating from the rooftop of the building I just exited from. When I looked up, I noticed two lads setting a mattress on fire. I could tell by their actions and voices that they were juvenile delinquents, and they used the 'F' word a lot throughout their mischievous giggling. They were doing this just as an old double-deck London Bus was slowing down to a halt beside a bus stop below them. I shouted up at them to draw their attention to stop messing about with fire, but the loutish lads both gave me the two fingers before throwing the burning mattress off the top of the house as it then landed on top of the bus.

The queue of people at the bus stop witnessed all this, but it didn't deter them from getting on the vehicle. And the driver must not have heard the thud because he took off with great speed down the street, while the wind acted as a bellows making the flames rise high above the packed bus. I could see the silhouettes of the passengers fading away, as the flaming Number 19 sped down the street in the twilight of the deep blue sky. I decided to do a U-turn on my bike and follow the bus in order to alert the passengers to the danger of the burning mattress. When I drew closer to the vehicle, while it slowed down at the traffic lights, I waved at the passengers and pointed up at the roof. Many of them turned their heads away and some of them covered their faces with a handkerchief as smoke was beginning to seep through the top deck.

Undeterred, I proceeded to follow the bus to the next stop. This time I got off my bike, stood up on the rear platform of the bus, and shouted into the lower deck, 'The roof is on fire! Get the fuck off the bus, now!' Two nurses dressed in midwife attire, shouted back at me, 'We don't care, we're trying to get to work, get lost!' while the bus sped off into a cove in the distance, its roof still blazing. I tried to follow it again, but I fell off the bike and hit my head on the pavement. When I stood up, my head was spinning and the street looked upside-down. I could hear the bus screeching to a halt in the distance, so I staggered with my bike to see what happened, as my vision slowly started to rotate back to normal. Parked on a quiet street and in flames, I could see the passengers sitting upright in their seats as if they were being cremated in the double-deck inferno. I could also feel the heat and see the silhouettes of the two midwives, who must've escaped the blaze, both standing on the street staring at the bus in a zombie-like trance. I shouted at them, 'Aren't you going to do something!' but they ignored me.

At this point, my head began to throb to the crackling of the bus inferno and the smell of human flesh being barbecued. I could also feel pins and needles in my legs moving up my body, so I slowly turned around and stumbled home in great pain. When I awoke the following morning, there was no mention in the news of the burning bus. My mother told me to give up drinking and see a doctor about that 'lump on your head'. 'Have you been in a fight?' she said. I told her about the burning bus, but she wouldn't believe me. She said I must have dreamt of it. Nowadays, it's all a distant memory, while I spend my twilight years a retired loner who walks an old Jack Russell along the seafront, reads the classics in bed at night, and tends to the garden during summer.

When I looked over the garden fence into my neighbour's yard when that old memory struck me, it wasn't a mattress that was smouldering, but a broken sofa. Maybe mother was right. Maybe I did dream it all up. I mean, what kind of people would risk their lives by jumping onto a burning bus for fear of being late for work and losing their jobs?

Edgar

As an honest, sane, freelance journalist, I feel compelled to tell this strange story that is no longer strange to most people in an era where the valorisation of deviance has reached its pinnacle. But after many months of deep research and dialogue with multiple eye-witnesses, I want to place before the Red-Pilled folk on planet Earth as clear as possible without any bias, a crazy series of events that occurred many years ago on the mean streets of one of America's most run-down sanctuary cities; a city where looting became a national pastime; a city where Christmas carol singing on street corners has been replaced by homeless people living in tents; a corner where long ago once stood impeccably dressed, Afro-American, high-school students singing the beautiful doo-wop symphonies of "Earth Angel" and "I Only Have Eyes for You"; in a city that shall be left unnamed to protect the reputation of the law-abiding folk who live there and are forced to contend with the random chaos from a criminal minority.

The story revolves around a boy I once knew, a borderline Savant-syndrome loner called Edgar, who had OCD tendencies in his diligent enthusiasm in making cuckoo clocks. His immigrant father, a widowed man, was a successful building contractor who grew up in a little town close to the Black Forest of Germany, before emigrating to the USA.

Edgar's Irish-born mother (also an emigrant) died when he was a baby. Before moving to the metropolis, the family used to live beside the harbour, and, on a windy night in early fall, Edgar's mother passed away with "a cruel fever that seemed to come out of the clouds", according to Edgar's father. But Edgar said the demons down under the ocean took her.

As a fellow loner boy who lived in the city, I knew Edgar, casually, as my parents owned a bar called The Raven's Nest, across the road from where Edgar lived with his father in a penthouse. Occasionally, I often met Edgar on the street and chatted to him for a few minutes. He was an only child; a skinny, short, po-faced kid with dark curly hair who spoke with a lisp. He was quite shy but friendly, always offering me a "Juicy Fruit" chewing gum whenever we met.

On one occasion when he offered some gum, a disabled man on a wheelchair across the road was being mugged by a hooded youth. When I pointed it out to Edgar, he seemed oblivious, as he held up an individually-wrapped gum and said it was such a waste of paper because the tinfoil-covering enveloped in the paper sufficed. I remember momentarily envying his innocence in an inverted world with all its mental turmoil and horror of existence. What relative solace it must be for one's mind to be occupied by wasteful wrapping paper on chewing gum while a fellow human being was being assaulted nearby (fortunately, the assailant ran away when the disabled man, dressed in a military jacket, punched him in the face).

Edgar also told me that he often found it hard to sleep at night for fear that some of the springs in his cuckoo clocks might malfunction. When I enquired how this might happen, he said: "A clock could 'cuckoo' at different times – the wrong times; skip a beat; run too slow or fast; the chain becomes loose; a part falls off; it might even *'quack!'* instead of *'cuckoo!'*, or it could stop completely." A digital clock would avoid all this, but from his teenage years,

Edgar   avoided   high-technology,   especially
computers. And he never had a cell-phone.

As for education: His aunt home-schooled him
and his father taught him business studies, as he had
an aptitude for mathematics and the logistics of
opening a small business. But unlike his father, he
had zero acumen in successful entrepreneurship
regarding saleable marketable products. He once
invented a rocking chair for retired sailors, with the
rockers facing sideways instead of forward. He
pleaded with his father to let him appear on a reality
TV show where entrepreneurs pitch their business
ideas to a panel of venture capitalists, but his father
forbid him and told him to break-up the chair and
make three cuckoo clocks with the dismantled wood.

Edgar obeyed his daddy and went to work on the
clocks, sitting beside his only friend, a black cat called
Annabell, named after his beloved mother. Edgar
spent most of his time making cuckoo clocks, a skill
that he was taught by his late grandfather, who told
Edgar that the cuckoo was a looter of other birds'
nests, in the same way that politicians loot the
treasury. Edgar also wrote short poems, on his
homemade Father's Day cards (hundreds of them),

typed on a retro portable typewriter. He was no William Wordsworth, but the clichéd poems he wrote on the cards were quite innocent, if not a tad childish: *"Daddy, you're not as old as the hills/In fact you're as fit as a fiddle/Thank God you are in good health/I love you more than life itself!"* Edgar would use Tipp-Ex whenever he made a typo. The odd time, he would sniff the white fluid to get a mild 'fix'. Edgar's father donated the cards to local charity shops and gave the cuckoo clocks as presents to his friends, work colleagues and business acquaintances.

As long as Edgar was busy at home and off the mean streets, his father was happy. And he would occasionally take his boy out onsite to watch how the architectural precast cladding concrete slabs for giant Brutalist structures are applied. Edgar would watch the men at work, while wearing his little Hi-Viz jacket and working men's boots. He once told me that when he glimpsed at the monstrosities made by the cement, he felt scared. He said he looked upon the brutal scenes before him—upon the bland features of the giant slabs—upon the grey walls— upon the beady-eyed windows—with a bleak pessimism of spirit. He didn't use those words but that is what he conveyed to me. He said the only time he got comfort onsite was when he fed pigeons on the roof of such a building. This annoyed his father who regarded these harmless noble birds as "rats with wings". His father had a theory that the high accumulation of pigeons' droppings on rooftops was the cause of damage to the masonry due to the high acid content acting like a corrosive, thus the mass of poop causing extensive damage and costs in repairs. He even speculated that if the bird poo could corrode buildings, then the acidic effects could do the same damage to their feet. "With large flocks of these winged rats living so closely together in small spaces, it's inevitable that the toe-less, stumpy vermin would spend much of their time standing in their own dung," he said. "And it's not just the birds," he added. "Many of downtown's buildings are slowly being washed away by the golden showers of homeless junkies. It is eroding thousands of historic buildings downtown, the exterior bases corroding with every spurt of urine. The acidic liquid is wreaking havoc on the architecture."

Despite his harsh comments, Edgar deeply loved his daddy. Although he was a conservative, he was also a Godless man and would often boast about his non-belief in a Creator. At a dinner party one evening celebrating Ronald Reagan's win to become US president, while talking about religion, he stood up at the table and said: "My deep faith in atheism is as strong as the Francis Scott Key Bridge, and robust as the invincible masonry and steel on the Twin Towers in New York City. It is a conviction that's written across my heart," as he pounded his chest before collapsing on the floor after suffering a fatal heart attack.

This saddened Edgar, but the upside was he left a handsome will to the boy. With this inheritance, which included a garage stocked with hundreds of boxes of working men's boots, hard hats and Hi-Viz jackets, Edgar opened a small store on the east-side of the city. The store was stocked with the boots, hats, cuckoo clocks, Tipp-Ex, and Father's Day cards. As the weeks turned to months, only a handful of mostly old people entered his store to browse; but alas, none of them bought anything. This was unsurprising for anyone with normal mental faculties, in a city with high unemployment and a preponderance of absent fathers. The only advantage of Edgar's store, like a books' section in a library, was its safety from any looting raid from city gangs. And in the week before Christmas Day, the pinnacle of looting season, Edgar planned to close-down his business. But on the night before the festivities, during a great looting raid on local stores, a group of elderly European men from the Austrian Kleptomaniac Yodelling Luddite Society, dressed in Lederhosen, were on walkabout downtown. All the men regarded themselves as 'recovering thieves' who were prone to 'fall off the wagon' if temptation arose. As most of the men were atheists and initially teetotallers, and could not join AA-type groups for recovery, as they didn't believe in a 'Higher Power', they instead turned to 'Yodelling Therapy' (YT).

This now-defunct therapy, which was quite expensive, was founded in the 1960s by a Swiss charlatan alcoholic called Ingmar Wolfgang Schnock. The motto of YT was, "A drunken man yodelling won't have theft on his mind," thus, it's "better to be a drunken yodeller than a habitual thief." And, in line with its motto, the YT entailed drinking lots of beer during meetings before a yodelling session, and this turned the formerteetotalling men into drunks. Worse: On that crazy night of looting, they picked the wrong city for a vacation to attend an evening with the International Alpine Wimoweh Association. While heading back to their hotel quite intoxicated after a night of boozing and heavy yodelling, one of the men broke into song, singing "The Lion Sleeps Tonight", while his fellow-yodellers backed him chanting the "a-wimoweh" verse. Suddenly, they saw Edgar's store, its windows smashed but no goods stolen from the shelves. Inside the store was a display of 50 cuckoo clocks, on top of their boxes, timed to "cuckoo!" at the stroke of midnight.

As their kleptomaniacal tendencies were triggered by the sight of the cuckoo clocks, they stopped singing and rushed into the store and started looting, packing the boxes with the clocks and other goods. They then shuffled out with boxes under their arms, as they broke into song again. However, a feral Scandinavian gang from a nearby neighbourhood saw the men walking quickly, so they stopped the men and robbed them, fleeing with the boxes, unaware of the bland contents inside, as they ran back into the neighbourhoods at five minutes before midnight. We will never know how those dudes reacted when they discovered the contents of the boxes. But it might have been devastatingly disappointing when, at the stroke of midnight as the boxes were being opened, the cuckoos, en masse and in flawless unison, emerged cuckooing from their clocks like an army of Jack in the Boxes. And the robbers might have subsequently experienced a double anticlimax, as they opened packets of Father's Day cards, working men's boots, and jars of Tipp-Ex.

Back at the store, Edgar stood weeping at the door as the cuckoo call, mixed with a cacophony of the gang robbers shouting "*MUDDA FUGGA!*" and "*SHEEEEIT!*" could be heard echoing in the distance. Edgar swore to never open a business again, despite continuing to make cuckoo clocks, and he spent the rest of his time rescuing injured, stumpy-legged pigeons from the revamped store converted into a sanctuary for legless birds. He would use the Tipp-Ex on the bird's damaged stump as a kind of makeshift Plaster of Paris, applying it heavily to protect the birds from further damage when the fluid hardened. As for the Austrian men: After a morning of hard hangovers, they bought a crate of whiskey and boarded a bus to the harbour, where they stole an old Galway Hooker, to sail back to Europe. But the boat sank during a storm before reaching the Atlantic Ocean, killing all the men on board.

Some years after those infamous events, like a ghost, I strolled around the haunts of my boyhood days in search of Edgar, finally bumping into him on Main Street. He looked quite shabby and was holding an injured pigeon in his hand, both its stumps covered in Tipp-Ex. He said there were rumours that some gang members found an odd use for the boots and cuckoos: The tops of the model bird heads and bodies were hollowed-out and pipe stems stuck into their rear ends to make crack-type pipes filled with Tipp-Ex fluid mixed with the melted rubber from the working men's boots. When these addicts got intoxicated with the substance, it was rumoured they would go out onto the street en masse like a zombie apocalypse, while singing, in perfect harmony, the "a-wimoweh" chorus, followed intermittently by a barrage of yodelling and cuckoo sounds. It was as if the ghosts of the Austrian men rose from the depths of the sea, and had possessed the wailing youth, as a form of revenge from the grave.

As I stood looking at Edger, in disbelief, he slowly walked away. He looked a bit unsteady on his feet, and I am almost certain I heard him quietly sing, "a-wimoweh a-wimoweh…". Could he also be possessed, I thought? Or did he and the gangs of youth sublimely hear the men singing on that crazy night as they ran up the street, thus internalising the song, which subsequently manifested and became triggered in the depths of the Id, usually around midnight, under the influence of Tipp-Ex/rubber intoxications as the solvent passes through the blood-brain barrier? Maybe it was a kind of collective consciousness awakening of an autonomous existence of a deranged egregore, or a manifestation borne out of a subconscious attempt to expiate their guilt of robbing the goods off the Austrian men. A subconscious bid to *erase* the shame of theft, thus endeavouring to *correct* their ways. Or could it be a phenomenon like the Tanganyika Laughter Epidemic of 1962: A mass psychogenic illness in Africa, rumoured to have occurred in a village near Uganda, in a girls' school, when the girls began laughing uncontrollably for weeks? And, God forbid, if such monsters from the Id spontaneously crossed over to future generations of selected groups by manifesting epigenetically from the DNA of their ancestors, a shared psychosis, if you will.

Perhaps one day some intellect greater than I will solve this mystery, unless, of course, the rumours are false. But if they are true, then rest assured there will not be gangs of young men from that neighbourhood with looting on their minds if they are yodelling while high on Tipp-Ex and melted rubber. I often wonder what Edgar thought about all this madness or if his mind was still more concerned with one of his cuckoos 'quacking' instead of 'cuckooing'.

The Ghosts of Hologram House

I live alone in the city, and one stormy night while lying in bed, I started to think of my late parents and how loving and caring they were to me whenever I was ill. As a young boy, I was a delicate child and was regularly sick with colds and sinus. My parents died many years ago, and they occasionally occupy my mind, particularly on stormy nights. My mother managed to reach the grand old age of 93 before dying of cancer, while my dad popped his clogs aged 81 after he suffered a brain aneurism. He came home from the bar one night and dropped dead in the hall by the stairwell. My mother rushed into the hallway and told me that his last words were, "Don't forget to put the cat out."

I am their only son, with my two estranged sisters, much older than me, living abroad since the 9/11 attack on the Big Apple. I moved to California and got a job in I.T. at a giant finance company, and I haven't seen my sisters in the past 10 years. I love them, but I don't like them. The feeling is mutual, as our political and social world views clash. I hate to admit it, but I find them stupid and boring. I used to be stupid too. Up till the age of 43, I was a complete moron and believed everything I heard on the news on TV or in the Press. And I looked up to doctors and scientists, like they were gods. I was a man of extreme stupidity, a dopy guy who thought I was an intellectual giant. And I was a moral coward and weakling, but thought I was brave. I was also superstitious, despite being an atheist. I avoided walking on the cracks on the pavement, which made me look like I was playing hop-scotch like a little girl. I was such a fool back then and deeply unhappy; unhappy, hypocritical, paranoid, sensitive, misunderstood, and lonely.

Then one afternoon while in church on the day of a friend's wedding, I had a Road to Damascus moment. I have no idea what caused it. I think it was something that the priest said triggered a deep feeling inside my soul. And my awakening further grew and grew when I discovered many of the myths I once believed in, which were exposed as fake on the internet. The internet also informed me of Hologram House, where I spent Thanksgiving Day with the hologram ghosts of my dead parents. This place is a five-storey building, west of Silicon Valley, where they produce holograms of dead singers and actors, amongst other characters.

The deal is straightforward: For $6,000, a person requests a meeting to interact with a dead person for a short period of time, in my case an afternoon, with such a deceased person(s) recreated into a hologram. I had to supply the company with old film footage, complete with sound, of my parents at family events. The company also required two written anecdotes at such family events, which they inputted into the narrative of the algorithms AI for my parents' hologram to respond to. The script was recorded by a male and a female actor, then the voiceover was digitally converted to that of my mother and father's voices.

The brain behind Hologram House was a movie buff technician who based the House's 'meet and greet' avatar experience on a 1970s' futuristic story about a highly realistic adult amusement park called Elbow, which featured three themed worlds: American Wild West; Medieval Europe; and ancient Pompeii. In these resorts, lifelike androids are indistinguishable from humans, with each programmed to act like the people who lived during such epic eras. To enter Elbow and relive a fantasy with such robots, a fee of $1,000 a day is required, where guests can indulge in sexual encounters and simulated fights to the 'death'. In contrast, with Hologram House, the experience is in a much smaller interior space, and the characters are, unlike androids, non-physical, less threating, and limited in scope (a sexual encounter would be like copulating with the wind).

When I arrived at the building on Thanksgiving Day, I was ushered into a room with a set table full of food and a glowing AI-generated fireplace with logs 'burning'. The piped music in the room was that of Nat King Cole softly singing some romantic song about chestnuts roasting. I sat down and my parents' holograms entered the room and sat opposite me. They both looked aged 70. I noticed the cushion on my mother's chair didn't flinch as she sat down, and I couldn't hug them as they were not physical. We said hello and how glad we were to meet each other on such a wonderful day. I was surprised they didn't say 'Grace' before the meal, as they always did when alive. Throughout the dinner we joked, laughed, and spoke about old times. I lamented on my seventh birthday and how our Great Dane, Tiny, overturned the table while we managed to save the cake. My Mom and Dad holograms laughed at this and sung "Happy Birthday" to me. Sometimes they responded the wrong way when I said something, as the AI could not distinguish between some homophones and semantics. When I told them I could've killed them the day they were late for my graduation, they just stared at me blankly in a defensive way. And when I told them it was 'guerrilla warfare' in the company where I worked while 'swimming with sharks', my mother nodded her hologram head and said monkeys and large fish can be quite aggressive. Then suddenly, Nat King Cole's singing was replaced by the Sex Pistols singing "Pretty Vacant", and my father's hologram began to malfunction, as he went into an incomprehensible rant, saying: *"You tell big John that his grave will be in my grave tomorrow. Tell him! Tell him now! Here we are and there you are and here we are a clatter."* Then, in Johnny Rotton's voice, my father sang: *"I've been away from you a long time/The birds are singing it is song time/The banjo's strumming soft and low/I know that you Yearn for me too/Swanee, how I love you, how I love you/My dear old Swanee/I give the world to be/Among the folks in D-I-X-I-/Even though my mammy's waiting for me/Praying for me Down by the Swanee/The folks up north will see me no mor/When I get to that Swanee shore."* Throughout his singing, my mom just stared blankly at me with a smile on her face. I stood up and left the room, as I couldn't take any more of watching this pair of ghosts in Hologram House.

As I was leaving, my dad stopped singing and, in his own voice, said, "What's for dessert?" to which my mom replied, "I...am...your...automatic... lover...automatic lover...I...am...". On my way out down the corridor, I passed by a room with the sound of a piano playing. The door, with a sign on it reading "An Afternoon with Liberache", was ajar, and when I peeped into the room, I could see a group of old ladies drinking wine, while watching the hologram of Liberace playing the piano. The women looked confused, as Liberace's voiceover was that of Lieutenant Pigeon signing the chorus of the 1973 UK hit, "Mouldy Old Dough". It seemed the avatars of my parents weren't the only ones having malfunctions, with the distant, creepy echo of my mother's voice down the corridor repeating, "I… am…your…automatic…lover…automatic lover…I am…". But I didn't seek a refund, as I wanted to exit the building as soon as possible.

There was something nightmarish about the situation. At one point while leaving the building, I had to pinch myself on the hand to see if I, also, could be a hologram. On my way home, I walked into a church and lit a candle for my parents and said a prayer for them. Across the aisle where I was praying were two old Mexican ladies queuing for Confession. They could've been holograms for all I knew. While on my knees, I regretted that I remembered my parents as two weirdo ghosts at a dinner table and not the sane loving couple I once knew. Also, I wondered was it right to project hologram performances of your parents or loved ones who are now dead without having obtained their express consent while they were alive? It was like a kind of spirit theft. However, the feeling of nausea was lifted when I left the church.

Outside the place of worship, I met the parish priest and told him of my hologram experience. He said he heard of a California pastor's Sunday morning sermon being beamed recently to a New Zealand congregation. Apparently, the pastor addressed the people at an Auckland City church via a three-dimensional image. The priest said he thought it was a good idea, as most priests are aged in their 70s and the Church finds it difficult to replace them when they retire or die, due to low numbers entering the priesthood. I told him that the problem with using hologram technology at Mass, is how can the holographic priest hand out Communion?" He replied, "I agree, but it can work for a sermon."

In the news the following day, there was a report on Hologram House, saying some staff member 'deepfaked' the inputs of the auditory programmes in the building the previous day after having a heated argument with the CEO.

The Busybody

I've lived beside the Bay Area all my life. On weekends, I get a little pleasure driving down to a late-night store near the Golden Gate Bridge to talk to an old friend who owns the store. There was also a boxing club near the shop where I used to train as a kid, but it has been boarded-up for years. I used to attend the club twice a week for sparring practice. I remember beside the ring on a shelf on the wall stood a chalk statue of the Sacred Heart watching us bashing each other. When you think about the nature of the sport, it's quite strange: a small community of men (or women) of various backgrounds and beliefs in a building, sweating, skipping, and punching each other to a pulp, yet hugging each other after a fight and setting aside their differences and remaining close acquaintances. But I digress.

The area at the store that I drive to, is a quiet place at night, with lots of parking spaces. I usually buy a few beers and have a chat with the owner, Floyd, who used to spar with me in the club many years ago. We always talk about the boxing champs from yesteryear. He said his father once met Rocky

Marciano. But on that fateful night three years ago, something bad happened to me that later turned out to be good. I drove down to pick up a frozen pizza for supper and parked my car in a 'mother-and-baby' space. When I got out of the car, a young man getting off his bicycle approached me. He was wearing a bicycle helmet, Lycra attire, Hi-Viz jacket and a surgical face mask. He took out his iPhone and started filming my car, especially the interior, driving plate, as well as the 'mother-and-baby' sign in front of the car.

"Are you all right?" I said to him.

"You can't park there. That's a mother-and-baby space. Can't you see the sign?" he said. I told him I had a bad back and that the parking lot is empty, except for us. He said the space is reserved for a woman of colour with kids, and not a white privileged fascist. "To hell with your bad, white hump. Now, kindly reverse out of there or I'll call the cops," he said. I asked him did he have any kids himself, and he said they were at home with their mother. "And if they were here with me now, you would be the problem. There's plenty of vacant spaces here this evening," he said, "and you might as well have pissed on this space."

I told him that only a sitzpinkler would say something like that. He asked me what the term meant, and I explained that it is a man who sits down to pee; a beta-male who has lost his manhood.

He said, "Well, I must admit, I happen to sit down while peeing and I'm proud of it. I bet *you* don't sit down. I can imagine the stinking stains on the marble on your bathroom floor." I said, "But what if you forget to sit down, what happens then?" "We've installed a WC-Geist," he said. It's a German-made device that lives under the seat, and when the seat is lifted, a voice orders you to sit down. You can get a WC-Geist fitted with your favourite voice-over."

I said, "Really – but don't tell me. I bet you've installed the recorded voice of your wife, right?" I then asked him when did he have that Urethra Eureka Moment on that Road to the Lavatory?

He said, "I read an article in a newspaper about research done at a medical centre. They investigated how body position during urination affects voiding time, maximum flow rate and post-void residual volume. They concluded that sitting has a more favourable urodynamic profile, allowing the bladder to empty faster and more completely. For men with lower urinary tract symptoms caused by an enlarged prostate – the sitting voiding position is preferable to the standing."

"Very interesting," I said sarcastically."

He replied, "I also read that an American professor of mechanical engineering, using a urination simulator and high-speed cameras, said he and a colleague did an investigation into 'splashback'. This is caused by urination gone astray, a theory that the professor presented at the 33rd annual meeting of the American Physical Society's Division of Urination Dynamics in 2012. The professor managed to explain what happens when urine leaves the penile urethra."

"I'm all ears," I said.

"The professor said a stream comes out but after between three and six inches it starts to break up into droplets," he said, "and that's where most of the problem comes from. The droplets start to impinge on each other, then you get what he calls satellite droplets and they splash-off at very large angles and this is what causes it to splash onto your toothbrush or around the sink, mirror, and floor." I told him that his exotic knowledge of urination makes quantum theory look like a walk in the park. I said to him that I must remember all that he said when I come home drunk one night. "And what about Number Two?" I asked, "is there a right way to do that one? Can't imagine standing up for that one would be advantageous. Your toilet talk is inspiring, but I have to go now; there's some shopping to be done. My advice to you is see the best shrink in San Fran, as I feel something might have happened to you in a parking lot during your childhood. Did mummy abandon you? Is that why you're so vengeful?"

The busybody looked at me with a morose expression. "Yes…she left me in a supermarket parking lot when I was a young boy, a year after my father left home," he said. Breaking into a monologue, he added: *I loved my mother. She would bring me to the playground and gently push me on a swing, while singing a lullaby; and during the summer, we'd head off to the beach and swim in the sea. She loved the ocean. Once she took me to a circus, the greatest show on earth. There were clowns and elephants and dancing bears riding bicycles. And a strange-looking woman in pink tights flew high above our heads. But there was something missing. I said to my mother: Is that crazy woman flying above our heads all that there is to a circus? She laughed at me and said I sounded like Peggy Lee. I never quite understood what she meant by that. She was such an optimist. Mother once said to me, 'I don't have to tell you things are good. Everybody knows things are great. It's ecstasy and love is everywhere. Everybody's working and they'll never lose their job. The banks will never go bust, shopkeepers don't need security, and the streets are safe to walk on at night. The government loves us. We know the air is fit to breathe and our food is fit to eat and all vaccines are safe, because doctors and scientists never lie. And we sit watching our TVs while the man on the telly tells us all is well, and it will end well. He never, ever lies because he knows things are great – better than great: They're bat-S.H.1.T-crazy great! We don't have to go out for a walk. We can sit in the house, and slowly the world we are living in is getting better all the time, and we can sit in our rooms and watch TV all day; and in summer, we can have our air-conditioning on full-blast when outside feels like the world's on fire.'* "I told my mother that I wasn't happy, and she said, *'Well, I can fix that. I don't want you to protest. I don't want you to riot - I don't want you to write to your local politician because I wouldn't know what to tell you to write. And being a little boy, you probably wouldn't know what to write. All I know is that first you've got to get happy immediately. You've got to say, I'm a HUMAN BEING, damn it! My life is wonderful! So, I want you to get up now. I wish everyone in the world would get up right now and go to the window. Open it, and stick your head out, and yell, 'I'M AS HAPPY AS HOWARD BEALE'S OPTIMISTIC TWIN BROTHER AND I'M GONNA BE EVEN HAPPIER TONIGHT!'"*

I told him that *my* mother was quite the opposite. She said the world is fallen and run by psychos. She was a moral woman who read the Bible every day. He told me that his mother didn't need a Bible to make her good. She was a Democrat activist and worked at night in the Burke and Hare Memorial Hospital, the "greatest institution on Earth". He said his mom was the hospital's accountant. She used to say, "A patient healed, is a customer lost". When I told him his mother must have been a psycho, he quickly took out a gun from his pocket and shot me. He then cycled off as I lay on the ground in agony from the wound. I managed to call the emergency service with my iPhone.

A female robotic-sounding voiceover answered the call. She (or it) said, "Hello, you've reached Burke and Hare Memorial Hospital. Please hold while you are connected to the next available customer support representative." The on-hold music was The Ink Spots singing, "I Don't Want to Set the World on Fire". When the music stopped, she said, "Thank you for calling. Please stay on the line. Your call is being connected to one of our operators. All of our operators are currently busy. Please hold, and we will answer your call as soon as possible." The song came on again and continued for a few seconds as I lay dying, then it stopped, with the voiceover saying, "All of our electrical ambulance vehicles are currently being charged, with one of them on fire at the hospital gates. If you need a callback from us, please dial 666, and we will contact you as soon as an EV is available; otherwise, please stay on the line and your call will be answered in the order it was received."

As I lay on the ground in a pool of blood, I wanted to say a prayer but had long forgotten the words of prayers. Luckily, a man in a pick-up truck saw me and rushed me the hospital where I spent three weeks in recovery. They never caught the little bastard who shot me, and who knows if he'll shoot somebody else who parks in the wrong place. While in hospital recovering, the man in the bed next to me, reading a book on theodicy, was the CEO of a big publishing company. We became friends and he commissioned me to write a book on my experience in the Faction genre, which is half fact, half fiction. It took me four months to write it, and it sold over 300,000 copies. It was entitled, "Car Park Blues". With some of the royalties, I bought the old boxing club beside the store and revamped it, with the help of Floyd. We managed to save many junkies and feral gang members from crime who now train there three times a week at the club. As for the 'mother-and-baby' sign at the store's parking lot: Floyd sent it to me as a present on the day I was leaving hospital. I've hung it on my laundry room wall and, with rust around the edges, it might one day make a good price as a vintage collectable sign.

Kingdom of the Moon

On Saturday night, JP sat slumped on his couch in a city apartment at the edge of Chicago City. He was watching a programme on the Easter Tridentine Solemn Mass, which took place in 1941 in the Church of Our Lady of Sorrows, a church that JP used to go to for Sunday Mass. JP watched this old documentary on TV while sipping a cup of tea, dozing off slowly to the sound of Gregorian chant.

Lying asleep beside his master was Chopper, a 10-year-old miniature English bull terrier, looking like a little baby shark covered in white fur. He was a tiny, food-obsessed dog with delusions of Great Dane grandeur. (Despite the little breed being prone to deafness due to the genetics of their coat colour, JP suspected Chopper could hear a fridge door opening from a distance of half-a-mile. He suspected this because one day while he was walking Chopper in the park, the dog suddenly stopped and pricked his ears. Some 15 seconds later, JP's mobile phone rang. It was his wife, who told him they were out of milk.)

As Chopper lay on the couch, his jowls sporadically fluttering on his crooked snout to the

Latin sounds of long-dead priests, JP's eyelids began to slowly sink. He had earlier been demonstrating in a city march against the destruction of the rain forests. Lying on the couch in a semi-slumber, he thought about his boring life: dull job in a dull office; dull work colleagues; dull relationship with his wife; dull, dull, dull. And despite having done very little of great excitement since his wedding day, he nonetheless suffered from the melancholy of having done all things. He found it hard to sleep and suffered bouts of anxiety that made him twist and turn in bed at night, keeping his wife awake. He also recently began having brief episodes of vertigo and had not ridden his bicycle in weeks. Blaming the pollution in the city, he tried to convince his wife to move to the countryside where they would travel the next day to view a small house in a quiet little estate down by the river.

JP was lying on the remote controls, half-dreaming to the rhythm of the TV's sounds. But no sooner had he closed his eyes, the TV was switched off. He looked up at his wife, a thin, pretty woman of 36 years, looking down at him. She had spent the whole day getting beauty treatments, but she was wearing too much perfume. She said, "I can't go with you tomorrow. I got a call from Dad; Mum is sick again. Can you go by yourself?" JP didn't have much contact with her mother but whenever he saw her, she looked healthy and fit for a woman in her late-50s. She was a theatre actress who once said she'd like to die on the stage while playing Hedda Gabler. JP felt like dying in the apartment playing Othello, but he slowly got up and yawned. It was 2am, and he and wife headed for the bedroom.

Early next morning, the streets in the city were quiet with the distant sound of a church bell ringing. It was late spring, and the sun was lukewarm, but the air was dry. Several tiny eco-cars beside the train station were plugged into charging-meters at the side of the road, and a homeless man sat beside the station's gate softly singing a song about Jesus loving him. The man, who was in his late-40s, was chubby and dressed like a hipster. He reached out his arms to Chopper and continued singing the song to him. The dog pricked his ears, tilted his head and wagged his tail, as if he was trying to understand what the man was singing. JP offered the man some money, but he refused and said a train was due and they'd better hurry up or they'd miss it.

JP and Chopper boarded the train for a little town some 35 miles away. Chopper started to drool when he saw two fat kids, sitting on the opposite seat, stuffing their faces with chocolate ice-cream, while an elderly woman with the children fiddled incessantly on her iPhone. She had a pierced nose and a Looney Tunes Road Runner tattooed above her ankle. The sun blasted through the windows as the train left the station. JP put Chopper on his lap and placed his sunglasses over the dog's sensitive eyes, which made the children laugh.

After one hour on the tracks, they were well into the countryside as he and the dog got off the train at a deserted station beside a river. In the distance, he could hear an out-of-tune choir singing a hymn. Farther up by the river, stood the little estate, surrounded by trees. The houses were half-built and deserted, with scaffolding around the odd, redbrick semi. He walked down by the river and passed by a small church where the choir was singing. Chopper, howling like a wolf, hobbled by the church. The pair walked farther on into the estate where they ambled around the houses.

At one of the houses, a young, Middle-Eastern-looking man, wearing a hoodie under a hi-viz safety jacket, was holding a sledgehammer and looking over at JP. "Are you buying a house?" he asked JP, in a perfect English accent. Chopper growled at the man. "Chopper! Stop that!" said JP, as the man stood back. "Sorry about that; it's the first time he's ever growled at someone," said JP, tugging at Chopper's leash. "Where is everyone?" JP asked. "Gone to the moon! It's Sunday," joked the workman. JP said, "I thought you guys worked on the Sabbath?" "Some of us do," said the workman. "How much does this house cost?" said JP. "This one's already bought; it's one of the better ones; got an orchard round the back," said the workman. "I love trees," said JP, "I can see how it was whipped up so fast." "It's got one little problem," said the workman. "Come round the back and I'll show you."

JP and the man walked around the side of the house and into the back yard, where a dozen apple trees stood in front of an old brick, chest-high wall with a tall iron gate in the middle. Over the gate, a wrought-iron sign read: 'Kingdom of the Moon'; underneath a smaller sign read: 'Dog Pet Cemetery'. Inside the cemetery stood 15 headstones, most of which had moss growing on them. JP spotted an inscription on one of the headstones which read: 'Boxer – 1913-1924; You lived through the Great War and were loyal to me till the end'. Other inscriptions showed the average dog died aged 11 and 13.

JP looked down at Chopper who was sitting at his foot. A horrible feeling of melancholy sunk deep into his soul, as he thought about losing that wonderful little rascal who thought he was Goliath. He said, "Why is it called Kingdom of the Moon?" "I think the man who built it was an astrologer. He died after the Second World War. They say his own pet is buried in there. Anyhow, it's a waste of land. We have to level it," said the workman, as he put down the sledgehammer and rolled up his shirt sleeves. He then took half a sandwich out of his pocket and placed it in his mouth.

"You're not seriously going to break up the headstones?" said JP. The man took out a large wad of notes out of his other pocket and held them up.

"For this amount of cash, you'd do the same. I'd rather bulldoze the place, but you'd never get a digger in here," said the workman with his mouth stuffed with bread, while he picked up the hammer.

"But you can't do that," said JP, "it's beautiful." The man turned his back on JP and started hitting Boxer's tombstone with the hammer. JP let go of Chopper's leash and jumped over the wall; Chopper hobbled after him, crawling through the bars in the iron gate. As JP tried to stop the man demolishing the headstone, the man dropped his hammer and fell to the ground; Chopper made a beeline for his half-eaten sandwich, which fell out of his mouth, and devoured it.

The man lay on the ground motionless; his eyes wide open, with blood on the back of his head. JP felt his pulse, but there was no movement and there was a smell of alcohol off his breath. Hanging out of his pocket was the wad of notes. JP stood with his hands shaking. He looked around at the deserted garden. Drops of rain began to fall. The sound of the choir could be heard in the distance.

JP took the money out of the workman's pocket; it was the first time he had ever stolen anything. He lifted up Chopper and quickly carried him back to the train station through a hazy shower of rain. As they arrived home, Chopper, with much effort, crawled up onto JP's lap, as he sat on the couch. His wife was still away, but her mobile phone was on the sofa. JP picked it up and clicked on her message menu. A message from a caller named Tom came up that read: "Really enjoyed today. If he's working late tomorrow night, let me know. I'll keep the bed warm! LOL!"

Instead of feeling sad and betrayed, JP was struck by a strange feeling of excitement. When his wife arrived home, she said she no longer wanted to move house, as her sick mother needed her around. JP pretended to look disappointed, and he never mentioned the phone message or the incident at the estate. All night long he was troubled by what he did at the cemetery. Should he have called for an ambulance? Called the police? Not stole the money?

At work the next day, JP couldn't concentrate. He could hear three work colleagues whispering behind his partition. When he looked through the gap in the desk divider, he could see a thirty-something man talking to two young women. JP could've sworn they'd mentioned his name. He quietly stood up and walked out of the office and went down to a corner cafe. It was run by a family of Hare Krishna's, and the owner, a little fat man called Malcolm, was cutting cheese behind the counter. He once told JP that in a previous life he had been a Roman emperor gladiator called Commodus (why is it never a Morris dancer called Herbert? thought JP). He served JP a dish of subji with basmati rice with a generous serving of homemade cheese curd chunks in a tomato sauce.

As he ate his lunch while reading all the morning's newspapers, he could see Malcolm at the back of the kitchen talking quietly on his mobile phone. Once again, JP thought he mentioned his name. He tried to put it out of his mind and went back to reading the papers. And despite no reports in any of the papers of a workman being killed, the headlines were the farthest news from JP's worries. They read: 'We share 60% of our DNA with bananas, say scientists'; 'Right-to-die man fights courts'; 'Robots to replace humans'; 'Police rescue man who spent a week trapped in handcuffs after 'autoerotic sex game'.

Far from the world of bananas, robots and autoerotic sex games, while working late one night two days after the cemetery incident, JP left the office and walked home. He worked on the edge of the city, and the journey to his apartment took him almost an hour. It was getting dark. The streets were quiet, with the odd person walking alone. He stopped at a nearby bar, where he could see, and just about hear, the TV news from a small, open window. He watched and listened to the main headlines from outside the pub, but there was still was no mention of a labourer being killed. He continued walking, taking the usual route through a long, quiet, cobbled-stoned laneway that curved its way round the corporate strip. He heard footsteps in the distance but couldn't tell if they were behind him or in a different street nearby. He knew it wasn't the echo of his own shoes because he always wore trainers. His heart started fluttering and his walking pace increased rapidly. The sound of a car could be heard coming up the street, as his vertigo started to act up again. He looked like a drunk walking home, but he stopped by a warehouse gate to catch his breath. A van drove quickly by and sped up the street. He remembered an eccentric, but harmless old electrician friend called Wireless he hadn't seen in many years who lived nearby. He needed to talk to someone, anyone except his wife. He turned a corner and walked up a long, moonlit laneway with bins lined against the walls, over which were metal balconies with fire-escape ladders hanging.

Wireless lived on a third-floor apartment in the middle of the lane. JP could see the light on in his place, but the main door was locked. He rang the bell several times but there was no answer. He could see someone pacing up and down in the apartment. He picked up a small stone and threw it up at the window. A young man opened the door and looked over at him. JP explained that he wanted to go up and see his friend and the man let him in. Walking up the stairs, he could hear the sound of a washing machine spin in one of the apartments. Arriving on Wireless's landing, he knocked on his door twice but there was no answer; as he was walking away, the door opened.

A dishevelled, middle-aged man with a shaved head and pencil moustache stood slouched in his dressing-gown, bloodshot eyes peering through spectacles without lenses, holding a glass of wine. "Wireless? Is that you?" said JP. Wireless turned around and walked back into the room; JP followed him. Inside Wireless's apartment, which was very warm, smelt of cannabis, stir-fry and smelly socks. A round table and chairs stood in the middle of the floor with a 40-watt lightbulb hanging over them. The room was full of books, tropical plants and old radios, many of which had wires hanging out of the back of them. JP wondered if it was Wireless's feet that stunk or the weird-looking plants. The walls were bare, painted hearing-aid beige and an unmade folded bed stood at the window with clothes piled up beside the headboard. On the windowsill stood a statue of Buddha wearing a baseball cap on its head.

The two men sat at the table drinking wine and talking about old times. Wireless told JP that all their old friends (which he referred to as "figments") from the past were pothead, welfare layabouts who spent half their time visiting hookers. He said he no longer believed in the reality of the external world. It all happened, he said, when he lay in bed one night and wondered if the moon existed if he turned his back on it. JP wanted to say, "blow it out of your rear-end, Wireless," but he kept his thoughts to himself so as not to upset his moonbat friend. Wireless had just come back from a two-year sabbatical in India and was thinking of buying some "figment-of-my-imagination goats" and moving to the "imaginary countryside" to make "imaginary cheeses" for export.

JP was glad to see Wireless hadn't changed too much. He was a peculiar genius but had obviously got many psychological problems. He told JP he once visited a psychiatrist and did a Rorschach test. In card after card, he reported seeing a woman's legs. Strangely, his mild descent into madness made JP feel relaxed. Wireless said, "Nobody gets their radio or TV repaired anymore. I haven't made a cent in years. If it wasn't for welfare, I'd be homeless. Modern technology has killed my business." JP said, "Have *you* ever killed anyone." Wireless looked surprised. "No. Have you?" he said. JP lied with a heavy heart, "Once." Wireless leaned forward, the dim light just about exposing tiny morsels of food stuck to his wirey, salt-and-pepper moustache. "What happened?" he said. "A man was kicking an old dog," said JP, "so I punched him; several times." Wireless said, "How did he die?" "He fell on the ground and banged his head," said JP.

Wireless was now looking at JP as if he was real, and not just a figment of his imagination. "Did the police arrest you?" he said. "No," said JP. "I ran off and never heard anything since. That was many years ago." Wireless leaned back and took a long sip of his wine. "I'd call that justice," he said. "Any man who kicks a dog deserves to be whacked. Forget about it; put it behind you." He took out a ready-made cannabis joint from his pocket and lit it. Taking a drag of it and inhaling deeply, he handed the joint to JP, who never smoked one before. He took a little drag from it and started coughing. It had no effect on him. He handed it back to Wireless, slowly stood up and said he had to go. As he was leaving, Wireless said, "Wait!" He stood up and slowly walked over to him and reached out his left hand and felt around JP's face, like a blindfolded person playing a 'guess who is it' game at a party. JP asked him if he was okay. "I'm... I'm fine," said Wireless. "Could you loan me 50 euro?" "Everyone I know is in debt," said JP. "I'll give it back to you when I get a job," said Wireless.

JP handed him the money and told him it was a gift. Wireless studied the note and smiled as if he was doing another Rorschach test. JP was glad to see

Wireless believed in the existence of cold, hard cash, even if the money wasn't his. Before leaving the room, Wireless called him back, fumbled in his trouser pocket, and handed him a small card. "Here; take this," he said. "Her name's Margaret. She does a lot more than physio. But don't tell her I sent you." JP was confused. He took the card and left the apartment.

The next day, he repeated the usual routine of buying papers and working late. On his way home one night, it started to rain. He walked into a brightly lit cafe for shelter and bought a coffee. A group of young people sat at a long table, talking loudly and sporadically looking at their iPhones. JP felt they were talking about him when their tone mellowed into whisper mode. The window behind the group was becoming fogged up. JP saw a figure outside the shop drinking from a cup, bearing a remarkable resemblance to himself, looking directly in at him. JP quickly finished his coffee and left the cafe but there was no man outside. He crossed the road and hopped onto a bus and went upstairs, which was empty. He looked down at the quiet city streets being washed away by the pounding rain.

A young man wearing a hoodie walked up the stairs and sat at the front of the bus. JP couldn't see his face, but his physical appearance was like that of the workman in the pet cemetery. JP sat nervously. As he got up to press the bell, the young man also slowly stood up and walked behind him. The rain continued to pound as JP got off the bus and walked quickly towards his apartment. The man in the hoodie walked closely behind him, the distance of the pet cemetery. When JP arrived at his apartment door, he struggled to find his keys. The hoodie man was getting closer, while JP quickly entered his apartment and closed the door and hid behind the stairwell. The hoodie man slowly entered the hallway and walked up the stairs. JP waited till the man's footsteps faded into the distance. He then got into the lift and pressed a button for the seventh floor. When the lift came to the fifth floor it stopped, and the doors opened. Outside, the corridor was deserted but well-lit. JP panicked, but the doors slowly closed, and the lift headed to the seventh floor.

On entering his apartment, he was greeted by Chopper, who then jumped up onto the couch and waited for his master. JP sat on the couch, his head sleepy and his legs tired. He quickly fell asleep and dreamt that he entered the pet cemetery on a sunny day and saw one of the graves dug up. At the foot of the grave stood the homeless man who was sitting at the train station. He softly sang the same song about Jesus. JP slowly woke up by rolling over on his side. He wondered about the homeless man and how horrible his life must be. How did he end up this way? And did he have any family? To think he was once a little baby safe inside his mother's womb. These thoughts disturbed JP and he remained awake all night.

The next morning, JP took Chopper for his daily walk. When he arrived home, his wife was still in the bathroom. Before leaving for work, he shouted at the bathroom door that he'd be working late, but the sound of the hairdryer inside muffled out his words, so he left for work. After work that evening, he went into a quiet bar in the city and ordered a drink. As he was counting the wad of cash, the small card that Wireless gave him fell out onto the counter. Over the telephone number and list of 'services' it read: "Madam Mags". Five beers later, he left the premises and rang Madam Mags. She was living in a basement flat a half mile from where Wireless lived. Before he got a chance to ring her bell, she answered the door and invited him in after he introduced himself. Inside the flat was clean and decked out in stylish, Scandinavian-type furniture. Mags sat on the bed, wearing a blonde wig, specs and dressed like a nurse. It was difficult to tell her age, but JP reckoned she was in her middle-50s. She had great legs, but her features were plain.

After he paid her 50 euro, she asked him what kind of sex he liked. He told her he didn't want sex but wanted to talk to her. 20 minutes later, Wireless was walking back from the shop with a bottle of wine when he spotted JP walking quickly in the opposite direction and looking around nervously as if he was being followed. For the next six nights, he visited Madam Mags after a drinking session and spent the remainder of the workman's money talking to her about the meaning of life. Near the end of the week, he was overwhelmed with a feeling of guilt and shame.

On midday at the weekend, he boarded a train and went out to the estate. When he arrived there, he saw the workman with a bandage on his head pushing a wheelbarrow. JP went over to the workman. They both looked at each other. The workman said, "It's you?" JP said, "I thought you were dead. Are you okay?" The workman said, "I was on my feet minutes after you left. It's only a scratch. Anyway, it's just as well you tackled me. The owner's wife convinced him not to demolish the cemetery. They're going to have it restored." JP said, "When I knocked you down and ran off, why didn't you call the police? I took your cash." The man stared at JP. "So, it was you who took the money. I thought I lost it." JP said he was sorry. "It's okay," said the workman. "I was glad you took it. I would've blown it all on booze. I haven't had a drink since the fall, and I don't intend to ever have one again." JP asked the workman for his name and phone number. "I'm going to pay you back every cent," he said, as he handed the man his business card. "Spend it wisely," he said.

As JP was walking away, the workman called him back. "You're Madam Mags?" JP had given him the wrong card. "Oh, sorry, that's a client of mine. Here, take this one," he said as he handed the man his own details on paper and took back Madam Mags card.

After he got home later that evening, JP put Chopper to bed. His old pet was beginning to move like a tired sloth. JP left his apartment and entered a church at the edge of the city. He had once seen the church's head cleric, who parishioners called 'Ron', at an anti-Capitalism demonstration near townhall. JP said some prayers and as he was leaving the church, Ron pulled up in a big, black Lexus. JP approached the car as Ron pulled down the door's window. "Can I help you," he said. JP asked him if he could have a brief chat about something that was bothering him. Ron asked him to get into the car. JP got in and started to tell his story. The cleric paused for minute before replying. His voice had an uncanny resemblance to JP's mother-in-law's tone, and this made him feel uneasy, especially because he seemed more interested in the precise details of his nightly visits to Madam Mags than in JP's relationship with his wife.

JP asked him if he and Mags were bad people who would end up in Hell. Ron said, "Who am I to judge? You may not know it, but you were looking for something good, and that's positive. You should follow your conscience and trust your instincts." He added that God "is a force", an "energy", and that

Hell didn't exist. He told JP to "get a good night's sleep and have a nice day." JP got out of the car feeling nauseous. When he arrived home, Chopper had died in his sleep. JP was deeply saddened but he never cried. Two days later, he paid the workman all his money back. He also bought an expensive sleeping bag and portable radio for the homeless man at the train station, but when he arrived there, the man was gone. A pretty teenage girl, who worked at the station's cafe, told JP he had died in his sleep some three days ago. She said the man didn't drink or smoke, and she fed him every day with sandwiches, cakes and coffee. JP felt sad but he was equally upset with the prospect of confronting his wife later that night about her affair. Before he spoke to her, she seemed in a fierce mood. He could hear her in the bathroom throwing something at the wall and saying, "bastard!" under her breath. He felt she was going to have a showdown with him, but when he approached her and asked her about the phone message, she broke down crying and begged forgiveness. JP hugged her and told her not to cry. He never mentioned his visits to Mags, and they spent the whole night making plans and talking lovingly to

one another. In the morning, JP changed the
tombstone wording on his will for an epitaph
inscription quoting from the Book of Job. But on a
small wooden plaque at the back of Kingdom of the
Moon, his little dog's epitaph read: 'Chopper.
Beloved Pet. Peace at Last.'

Albert's Toe

The canal stunk like a circus train had de-railed inside a giant sauna. But circus trains never came Albert's way, as he sat sipping a cup of tea at the window of his little bedsit in London's Eastend. Outside, he could see the murky waters beside the old railway line across from where he lived. He was waiting for the roar of the early morning train on its 200-mile journey up north where old people still call each other, "Chuck", "Mate", or "Love". With his razor-sharp 4-H pencil and crumpled-up loco register, Albert would take note of the train's arrival and speedy departure.

At the age of 51, Albert wasn't blessed with a handsome face or strapping good shape. He resembled the 1940s' screen Hollywood actor Peter Lorre. But the big toe on his right foot was a little stunner. That's what his chiropodist once told him. "I believe this bunionless, cornless, fungaless, goutless specimen of hallux to be a digit of supreme perfection, free from ingrown abnormalities and protruding proudly like the marble head of Apollo from the Mausoleum at Halikarnassos," she said

while she meticulously filed his toenail. "Of all the
toes that crept through my clinic over the past forty
years, none of them are worthy to walk in your right
shoe," she added; she also remarked that his left
kneecap was quite attractive, too, but it was no match
for his right toe.

Albert left the foot doctor's clinic that day with a
spring in his stride. He had buck teeth, was short, fat
and never dated a woman. His late parents left him
enough money to get by for at least 20 years and this
was of great help, as he suffered brief periods of
melancholy and found working with people difficult.
His highlight of the week was strolling down to the
butchers for two lamb chops and a chat with the local
butcher. The butcher was a tall man called Toby, who
wore a baseball cap covering his bald head. He spoke
a lot about trains and, as he chatted to Albert, he
chopped cutlets off the rack of lamb with great
precision. Albert noticed a scar on Toby's hand that
held the meat, which ran across the tops of two of his
fingers. The sight of the raised cleaver scared Albert,
as he was a bit squeamish to blades chopping meat.
In the evenings, he got some comfort from reading
the poems of Philip Larkin, knowing there where

many people more miserable than he was. He also read a lot about trains but knew the aversion the fairer sex had for anything locomotive-spotting. Still, there was hope: his beautiful right toe. And what good is a beautiful toe if it's covered up and never exposed to be complimented?

This got Albert thinking, as he sat at the kitchen window in his little ground-floor bedsit. The kitchen, which was untidy but clean, was lit at night by a 60-watt bulb. Sitting by the window under an old cuckoo clock and feeling miserable, Albert finally decided to go into town and chat up a woman - a mature woman attracted to men's toes. Wearing a white turtleneck, he dressed himself up in a brown chalk-stripe suit and got a blade and made his right cowboy boot into an open-toe in order to expose his best feature. Spotless clean and carefully manicured, Albert slipped his stockingless foot into the boot and headed out the door and far away from the local bars. It was early evening and the sun began to set after a passing rain shower.

Albert approached a city pub called The Toad's Rest, on the corner of Hatchet Lane. Two dishevelled-looking men in their mid-forties were standing outside the pub smoking. Both were staring at their reflections in a rain poodle as if they were awaiting execution. In the distance, a church bell rang. Albert entered the pub and walked up to the bar. The lighting was dim and most of the wooden decor had not changed since the late-1950s.

Three middle-aged men with morose expressions sat at separate tables, and one tall woman was sitting at the end of the bar reading a magazine. There was something of the prehistoric cave about the men, and they all wore female-repellent wear and looked like they fell off a collapsed Ferris wheel and survived. Two of the men clutched their beers, with one eye on their iPhones and the other on the woman at the bar; the other man was reading a newspaper with the headline, 'Horsemeat Scandal Boost For Butchers'.

An elderly, tall, thin barman resembling a Victorian undertaker, was dressed in retro tux-attire complete with dickie-bow. He stood at the top of the counter drying a glass and was quietly humming an old song called, "If I Died An Old Maid In The Garret". He seemed to be getting a mild sadistic pleasure from this as he gazed at the woman with the corner of his eye. She was no more than forty. On the counter beside her were a glass of red wine and a mobile phone. She wore sunglasses, navy corporate clothes, silk gloves, high-heels and looked very film noirish. She also wore what looked like a black, shoulder-length wig. Albert sat beside her and ordered a small shandy with ice. The woman continued reading the magazine, only glancing once at Albert, while he fumbled for cash in his pocket. When he sat down beside her, she crossed her legs, and the odd patch of black stubble protruding from her skin-coloured pantyhose was noticeable. Five minutes had passed and neither of them said a word.

The barman changed tune and began humming, "Only The Lonely". Albert ordered a pint of lager, to work up a bit of Dutch courage. He glanced up at a glass case behind the bar containing a stuffed dove, that seemed to be looking down at him. He then rested back and slowly crossed his legs, exposing his right toe, jutting out from a well-worn cowboy boot. The woman stopped filing and, tilting her glasses, looked down at Albert's foot. "Has anyone ever told you you're stunning?" she said to his toe, in a deep, seductive voice. "Yes," said Albert, with a chuffed expression. "My chiropodist has marvelled at the perfection of this little piece of hallux anatomy that up to now I have kept hidden from the public." "Can I touch it?" asked the woman. Albert smiled and nodded his head.

As the woman felt his toe, the barman stopped humming and glanced at the pair of them with a puzzled gaze. "Can I take a photo of it and send it to my friends?" she asked. "No problem," said Albert, "but don't take a shot of my face." The woman bent down, her face flush with Albert's toe, and took several selfies of her and the foot. Albert, who rarely drank alcohol, was getting a bit tipsy and tried hard not to giggle. He guzzled on his drink as the woman looked like she was sending the photos to her friends. For the next 15 minutes, the woman stared at Albert's toe, never once looking at his face. And when Albert tried to make conversation, the woman would press her finger to her lips and say, "Shhhh!"

At this point, Albert knew he had to face reality: she was only interested in his big toe. "I wish you'd talk to me," he said. The woman looked at Albert and said, "Do you mind if I draw a face on your toe?" Albert nodded his head in despair. The woman opened her handbag and took out an eyeliner pencil.

"This will only take five seconds; do you mind?" she said, with a sense of urgency. "If it makes you happy, sure, take as much time as you want; I wouldn't want you to have to look at my mush all night," said Albert, as he folded his arms and pursed his lips like a sulking child. The woman drew two eyes, a nose and a mouth onto Albert's toe. The barman stroked his chin and shook his head in bafflement. Two men in the bar pointed their phone-cameras at the pair. Albert was getting annoyed, but he was lonely and felt that he'd rather her go on romancing his toe than to have to make it through the night alone without her. And while she put her eyeliner back into her handbag, she looked at Albert again and said, "There's just one more thing."

She ordered a straight whiskey, then took a tube of adhesive and a pair of scissors out of her handbag. After she paid for the short, she cut a tuft of hair off her wig and dipped some tissue paper into the whiskey and started to clean the top of Albert's toe. She then dried it, rubbed the adhesive onto the top, then stuck the hair onto it like a little doll's wig. "If I talk to your toe, will you wiggle it so as to give the impression that it's responding to me? I know it

sounds crazy, but will you do it?" she asked. Albert
stared at her in disbelief, as she said to his toe in a
lustful voice, "Let me introduce myself: my name is
Toni. Do you come here often, halluxilicious?"
Silence. She quickly looked at Albert, who nervously
took cue and wiggled his toe. "Yes, I've been here
before on many an occasion," answered the woman
in a squeaky, babyish voice. "I think I've just met the
perfect sole mate," said the woman, reverting back to
her normal voice. "Would you like to come over to
my place for some foot-stomping, au-toe-roticism?"
she added. In a babyish voice, the woman again
answered her own question, saying, "I'll tow the line
for you anytime, Toni baby."

The men in the pub began laughing, but Albert
could see the barman looking cross. He knew there
was trouble a foot if the crazy woman kept up this
corny conversation with his big toe. "Enough of this
silly kowtowing to my foot, young lady!" said Albert,
as he lowered his leg. "I think it's best if we stop this
ridiculous game." The woman sadly looked down at
Albert's toe retreating into his boot like a turtle's
head withdrawing back into its shell. "I'm sorry if
your Achilles' heel is an exclusive fetish for male toes,

but you'll have to look elsewhere, as I'm looking for a woman who'll love me, not my toe. Anyway, what kind of name is 'Tony' for a woman? Good riddance!" he said, as he stood up and staggered out of the bar. Outside, he could hear Toni shouting, "It's spelt with an 'i'!"

Albert quickly walked away from the pub and lurched slowly in the rain through the little city laneways and under the canal bridge before arriving home soaking wet. He put the kettle on and sat on the stool looking out the window at the rain. After five minutes, the kettle started to whistle. Albert looked down and caught a glimpse of his big toe sticking out from the hole in his boot. The 'wig' was wet and had fallen to one side and the ink from the eyeliner was streaming from the 'eyes'. Albert began to see the funny side of this. He started chuckling but the laughter grew louder and louder till it reached fever pitch while there was a loud knock on his door. Albert stopped laughing. "Yes?" he cried. Silence. In the distance a train could be heard approaching. As Albert stood up, a louder four knocks on the door once again. A neighbour's door could be heard opening upstairs.

Albert slowly walked over to the door and opened it. Outside, Toni was standing holding aloft a butcher's meat cleaver. She was out of breath and there was mutilation in her eyes, as eyeliner streamed down the sides of her face. Her wig was tilted to one side revealing half her head, which was shaven, and her clothes were soaking wet, dripping onto the floor. She must have been over six-foot-four in height in her stilettos, and her lopsided wig and skinhead accentuated the menace of her piercing gaze. She pushed Albert back, stepped into the kitchen and said, in a diabolical, theatrical delivery, "Never fear, little one; it is not you that I've come for." The train's horn blasted as it approached the house, causing Albert's head to spin as the mechanical bird emerged from the clock squawking its two-note call, *"Cuckoo! Cuckoo!"* Albert yelled, "Help!" then he passed out in the middle of the kitchen floor.

The next day, he woke up in a hospital ward bed, his right leg resting on two pillows with the big toe missing. Despite having no toe, he could feel the digit was still attached to his foot and felt it was sporadically being jabbed by an invisible metal nail. He looked around the room, which reeked of an unpleasant chemical stench. It was early morning but still dark outside on a damp, April 1st. He could see a moth fluttering at the top of the tall window trying to break through and fly out to the street. Albert could also see the stars in the night sky from the window. On either side of him, two white-haired men lay asleep in bed like corpses; across from him, three younger men twisted and turned in their beds, one with his mouth wide open. The scene reminded Albert of a Larkin poem called, 'The Old Fools'. If only he had stayed at home last night, none of this would've happened. And would that deranged Toni with the cleaver wield that deadly weapon again on some poor, toe-dependent stooge searching for love?

Albert felt his own futile quest for love was over. As his mood was falling from a great height towards the abyss of despair, he looked over at the window and wondered what floor the hospital ward was on; and could he get up and walk that far before making the fatal jump? The old man in the bed next to him started to whisper a prayer. Albert knew the man was worse off than he, and he was struck with an overwhelming sense of guilt and shame because of this. Suddenly, his thoughts were interrupted by someone coughing at the door. A pretty, middle-aged, slim nurse entered the room and checked on the two old men. Albert pretended to be asleep, but he could see her through the corner of his eye. Slowly walking across the floor, she checked on the three younger men, wiping the drool from the one in bed nearest the window. Albert was hoping she would leave the room after this, but she walked over to him and checked his foot. With the bedside lamp shining on her face and illuminating her sallow, soft skin, she slightly resembled Toni, but her hair was fair and she was a few years younger. Pulling up the bed sheet, she started staring at Albert's left kneecap...his 'attractive' kneecap. Albert shouted, "Get away! Leave me alone!" and quickly jumped out of bed and hobbled towards the other end of the room, where he stumbled on the floor and smashed through the window falling from two storeys and landing on a rubber inflatable dinghy being towed by a truck on the road below. The nurse ran over to the shattered window and screamed as the truck came to a screeching halt half-way down the street.

The next day, the midday sun made the big garden of the hospital shimmer as it radiated through the double-glass doors of a private room where Albert was slowly waking up in another bed. The room was sparsely furnished. An electric clock on the wall struck 3pm. Albert's body ached all over and his right arm and left leg were held aloft in plaster of Paris. He thought, 'I have nothing left; my strength is rapidly fading.' Outside, a young, bearded man wearing dungarees, perspiration glistening on his face, was pruning a bush of thorns. Albert closed his eyes and prayed for strength.

Five minutes later, a petite nurse of Filipino origin in her mid-forties, entered the room. She stood beside the bed and read Albert's chart. She was subtly attractive, had long, dark hair tied in a ponytail, slightly blotched skin and wore no make-up. Albert opened his eyes and groaned, "What happened?" The nurse looked at him with a warm smile and said, in perfect English, "You've had a bad fall and broke some bones, but you should fully recover in five months' time. You've been here two days. Can I get you anything? Are you hungry?" Albert thought for a few seconds. "No thanks," he said. "Well, if there's anything you need just press the buzzer by the side of the bed and I'll come to you," she said, while walking towards the door. "Wait!" said Albert. "Can you get me a book on Philip Larkin's poems?" The nurse looked surprised. She smiled and said, "You like poetry?" Albert nodded his head. "I like Larkin, too, but I prefer G.K. Chesterton; have you read him?" Albert shook his head. "I have some books in my locker; I'll be back in a minute," she added, as she left the room.

This brought a smile to Albert's face, despite the aches and pains. When she returned to Albert, she told him her name was Ruth, sat down beside him and briefly explained what had happened after he fell. She then recited Chesterton's, 'A Prayer in Darkness'. Six weeks later, Albert was discharged from hospital with crutches. Toni had been sent to prison. Forty male toes were found in the lunatic's apartment at the bottom of a freezer, all individually wrapped and labelled in small plastic bags. Detectives said that person met the other thirty-nine victims at the beach and in public swimming pools. Albert, who was the last victim, made a full recovery and started dating Ruth, who got him a job in the hospital kitchen preparing vegetables. And she arranged for him to have fitted a cosmetic, prosthetic toe, which

Albert jokingly called, 'Hallux II'. They got married two years later and bought a house down by the canal. On Wednesday's, Ruth would buy Albert two lamb chops from his favorite butcher shop. But *he* would never set foot inside that place again.

Times Square on a Wet Afternoon

I must've read half of this cosmic book last night. Did you know that there is a volcano on Mars three times the size of Everest? I bet you didn't know that. It's called Olympus Mons. I wonder what the mountaineers of the past would've made of that. A middle-aged guy like me can hardly climb the stairs.

But in the past, some of these guys climbed mountains wearing a pinstripe suit while smoking a pipe. They probably flossed their teeth with barbed wire and slept in a giant handkerchief tent under the chilly moonlight. But back to the solar system: Did you know that Saturn has 82 known moons…and counting. Speaking of counting: Last night, I must have counted a million sheep, but I still couldn't fall asleep. I suppose things could be worse. I wonder if insomniac spiders count imaginary flies getting caught in their webs? The sight of a spider on the ceiling above my bed occurs every seven or eight weeks, and if my ceiling was made out of steel and I had a flame-throwing drone, I'd incinerate the little bastard. Only joking. Of all the creepy crawlies, spiders give me the shivers. There is something alien about them. But I was never cruel to animals or tiny-legged creatures. Instead, I got out of bed and gently placed the head of a sweeping brush under it, then placed the little fella safely outside my window ledge. The thought of one scaling down its silk web rope like a Navy Seal during the middle of the night and landing in my mouth as I sleep reminds me of what happened to an astronaut in an alien movie I once saw many years ago. He peeked into a pod and a crab-like creature jumped out and raped his face through his mouth. However, what struck me again the other night when I reached up the brush to the ceiling to catch the little alien, was: Do spiders think about things? Perhaps they're the lucky ones and are not too conscious like us. Consciousness can be a curse. I bet there's no unconsciousness in Hell. Imagine that: an eternity of conscious suffering. It's such a pain being stuck here. And *sooo* boring. I'm reminded of a Hitchcock movie where a gammy-legged Jimmy Stewart sits in a wheelchair in a little room all day, while his beautiful girlfriend pays him visits and keeps him company.

I once had a pretty girl, but she left me after my fall. Guess she didn't want to look after me. To be honest, I was glad to get rid of her. She never stopped moaning and wanted to watch TV all night. She kept saying I didn't understand her. That's true. But she didn't understand herself; always moaning. I once said to her, "You've corrected me four times today, did you know that?" To which she replied, "Five times... and this makes it six." In the end, she packed her bags and headed south to Baton Rouge to live with her sister and her two cats. She used to have three cats, but one of them died and she had it cremated. On the day of the scattering of the ashes into the Mississippi River, a strong wind blew the cat's remains over a passerby's Golden Retriever, whose fur instantly turned grey. It made the dog look a German Weimaraner with a medium coat. Poor dog. I love dogs. I bet the Retriever didn't know he was covered in dead cat dust. Dogs are so faithful. A prison doctor I know said when the wives or girlfriends visit their partners in jail, the first thing they ask is, "How is the dog?" He also said that when an offender is imprisoned for cruelty to a dog, he must be placed in solitary confinement for fear of attack from fellow prisoners.

When it comes to fidelity, pooches are the tops. But don't take my word on it: A friend of mine living in Portland has a cat and a dog. Last fall, during the heavy rains, his roof leaked so bad, a foot of water covered his entire floor. The cat left the house for a few days, but his dog stayed with him. When the mess was cleaned up a few days later, the cat returned. I hope my ex-'cat' doesn't return when I'm out of this plaster. Things could be worse, that's for sure. I often wonder how prisoners cope with being caged-in all day. I wish this pain would go away. The drugs don't work anymore. I'm going to have to ask my doctor to prescribe morphine. And it's not just the leg pain. The constant noise outside triggers my tinnitus, even though my hearing is bad. Man, I feel old. Did you know Americans are growing older, according to a recent census, which indicated that between 2010 and 2020, the number of people over the age of 55 grew by almost a third. Currently, life expectancy for men is 77 years and 81 years for women. Men probably die younger because they can't take any more complaining.

Anyhow, ageing sucks. So far, I've managed to retain all my own teeth and haven't lost my hair. I remember the first signs of ageing when I reached 45. In the years that followed, I would frequently fall asleep on an armchair while reading a book. Then came the Male Menopause, followed by panic attacks; back aches; inflamed knees; gout; sore hips; stiff neck; enlarged prostates; erectile dysfunction; too many treks to the bathroom; loss of short-term memory; senior moments; loss of short-term memory; hearing loss; poor eyesight. The ageing male might feel young at heart, but his bodily 'downstairs plumbing' is Victorian and prone to occasional leakage, while all upper body muscle heads south and melts into one big sack of blubber. Standing cryogenically frozen and naked while looking in the bathroom mirror at myself, I look like a giant, pealed pear. All that belly fat. Even if the flab shifts, it'll sag and look like a bloodhound's lip. What woman would be turned on by that? Even if you're a married man and not wealthy, your wife will be smiling, in the comfort of knowing that the chances of you committing adultery with a younger pretty woman are zero to minus zero. You're more likely to get a heart murmur than a hot momma. But I digress.

Those damn sirens on Times Square drive me nuts. I'm so used to them now, I can tell the difference between an ambulance and a cop car. I've lived in this garbage alleyway apartment off Times Square all my life, and every time I'm bed-ridden, everything becomes... magnified... or is it amplified? Anyhow, I don't seem to notice everyday sounds when I'm well, but now, light rainfall sounds torrential; a soft breeze sounds like a storm; doors closing sound like they're being slammed. I'll never ride an e-scooter again, that's for sure. Give me the subway any day. I'll take the risk of being mugged. I'm unfit for scooting around and falling down at my age, that's for sure. Even my breathing sucks. It must've been all those wasted poolhall nights inhaling second-hand fumes that eventually caught up with my lungs. But it could be worse: Had my parents not left me this apartment before retiring to Florida, I'd probably be sleeping on the streets. I'm glad I escaped that. Just imagine: lying in a tent with a leg in plaster of Paris, somewhere where even rats won't scurry. And those long winter months; huddled up in a cardboard box at minus 10.

That happened to my old friend Woody, two weeks after his parents topped themselves. Poor, Woody. Where could he be now? Woody was the unfortunate spawn of the dreaded Boomers; conceived at Woodstock. He never had a chance. Woodstock. All those years ago when two Deadhead parents sired Woody; well, the male Deadhead did, to be precise; he was a biology student dropout. **He** used to be in a jazz band, and he played the piano. When the band broke up, Woody and his dad managed to hoist the piano up to their fourth-floor apartment. But over the years, woodworm ate half the legs off the instrument, and some of the keys didn't hit the chords. So, in the dead of night, Woody's dad threw the piano out the window. Woody said when it hit the ground below, the final chord sounded like the end of The Beatles' song, "A Day in the Life". In grammatical terms, he said, it sounded like a period, followed by a cacophony of dogs barking and cats screeching in the alleyway below. And somewhere in the distance he could hear a baby cry. Woody's dad was also a notorious junkie and a special kind of degenerate. Woody once told me: "Tom, don't tell anyone this, but when I was a kid, dad tried to sell me to a pimp living on Seventh Avenue, but mom wouldn't let him do it. Dad said he wasn't wrong as we all evolved from apes and free will and morals don't exist. It would be no different from a sack of atoms selling a sack of atoms to another sack of atoms."

Woody also said that during the summer heatwave when his dad didn't have a dime, he would stand outside a downtown gin joint where he'd scoop-up some discarded weed from the floor of the bar's cellar. The bums who frequented one of the bars were mostly stoners and, before entering the den, they would often throw a joint butt they were finished smoking through the pavement iron gates where the beer barrels are lowered when delivered. The butts would land on the cellar floor beneath the exterior of the pub, out of reach for anyone to retrieve them with their hand. But Woody's dad had an ingenious way of fishing them up. During a summer heatwave, he would peal some of the hot, melting tar off the road with his penknife, roll it into a little ball, and press some fishing line through it. He would then lower it through the cellar gates, where upon touching the butt, the tar-ball would stick to it, thus enabling him to raise it back up. Sometimes he'd retrieve a dozen butts in one evening and make a big joint out of them all from a discarded page of the New York Times. There were other times out of sheer desperation, he'd shave off his beard, wear a pair of shades and dress up in a nun's habit that he got from a defrocked nun he once knew. Holding a white stick while shaking a fake collection box containing a few washers, he'd enter a bar where the drunks would donate change and probably forget they ever did it the following morning. The white collection box he rattled read: 'St Mary's School for the Blind', a place that didn't even exist.

Woody's dad would have done anything to stimulate his lust for a fix. He also drank a lot of spirits to keep him awake while doing the drugs. And when he woke up in the morning, before going into the bathroom, he'd make a B-line for the deli and by a baguette. When he got home, he'd cut off both ends of the bread roll and urinate into the top end, while the distilled Jack Daniels would slowly flow through the bread and drip into a paper cup. Woody said his dad would get half a cup whiskey from every pee. He and his wife were polluted beyond words, and they both had terminal health problems which made them quite irritable. They were always fighting with Woody. And he was prone to self-harm by damaging his arms with his sharp fingernails. During arguments, Woody would sometimes spin a vinyl of Chet Baker to drown out the shouting so as the neighbours wouldn't hear. That Baker LP had more scratches on it than Jupitar's moon Europa. It sounded like eggs frying on a pan to the tune of a trumpet and screaming junkies.

Woody's parents lied to him when they told him they owned the two-bed apartment on the westside of the city where the three of them lived. I remember being there once. The place stunk of weed and there were flies buzzing all around the room. Beside the main door, an old macaw parrot called Jerry was standing on a wooden perch. Every couple of minutes he'd screech expletives, mostly the 'F' word. I remember him screeching in a bad-tempered voice, *"Where's my f*****g reefer!"* and other such words as *"Stupid bitch!"* in Woody's dad's voice as well as *"Asshole!"* in his mother's voice. His voice sounded like Woody's father. As for the floor: George Harrison's guitar would've wept a river, the bathroom had no mirrors on the wall, and the tub was overflowing with empty beer cans. But it was the stale stink of cannabis that bugged me the most.

Woody once stole some of his pop's skunk, and when he found out Woody stole it, he threatened he would donate the estate in his will to some vegan group after he died. This pissed-off Woody, big time. He had planned to take his own life, but in the year leading up to his parents' deaths, with inheritance on his mind, he was never as kinder to them after eavesdropping on the pair discussing a suicide pact. They were convinced that they were infected with worms, slowly eating away at their organs. As they tearfully whispered about it, Woody, in an adjacent room hoping to speed things up, played the Peggy Lee classic, *Is That All There Is?* Indeed. Is that all there is? I sometimes wonder. Anyhow, after the pair later met on the ledge of the building and the ghastly deed was done, Woody was evicted and hounded for enormous debts his parents owed in rent arrears. With his great expectations shattered, Woody said, *"The bastads! They 'Miss Havishamed' me! She even wore her wedding dress when they jumped. And all I got was a lousy box of jazz shit and a statue of*

Buddha made of chalk." In a fit of rage after he got
the items, Woody kicked the head off of the Buddha
statue and spat on the box of LPs. He then went up
to the same rooftop of that fateful leap and fed the
pigeons. He loved those birds more than his folks. He
also said he felt guilty that their deaths gave him great
relief; it was like he escaped from being devoured by
their demons.

Poor, Woody. I wonder where he is now. It's been
eight years since I last saw him. I started to distance
myself from him when he pestered me for loans of
money to pay off his parents' debt, but he ended up
drinking it all. Some Irish dude introduced him to
Guinness, and he couldn't get enough of the black
stuff. A welfare cheque and stout were the highlight
of his week, as he breastfed his frayed copy of
Kerouac's '*On the Road*'. For someone who
graduated with a first in American literature, his
dreams of becoming the next great 21st-century
Kerouac were all in vain, and quite outdated by 40
years. If only Woody's mother could've loved him
the way Jack's mother loved *her* son, he could've
given something back to the world. All I ever got
from him in lieu of payback on loans was the box of

jazz LPs his parents left him. I sometimes play the easy-listening stuff when I'm in bed reading my astronomy books.

Last month, there was a full moon, and I remember wondering if Woody was lying in a tent somewhere downtown, scratching his arms with his razor nails, while the universe just kept rolling along. I decided to look for him after I sold, for $10 grand, one of the rare jazz LPs he gave me. But I felt guilty about getting such a high price and wanted to share half of it with Woody. I remember there was a lively boulevard near where he used to live, with bars and pool halls, and beside it was a strip of homeless people living in tents in an alleyway. I taped a Baker tune on my phone, the scratched track, and cycled down to the area to see if I could find him. The night was cold, as I rode by the tents with the phone playing the track. I did a U-turn at the top of the lane and cycled back, ever so slowly, below tenement fire escapes on either side, illuminated by a great white orb high above in the night sky. I noticed how dirty the area was at the bottom of the lane where the pavement was littered with rubbish. But as I progressed to the top end, the tents and ground looked a lot cleaner. I could see the silhouettes of some of the people inside tents, mostly single figures but sometimes in pairs: one couple playing cards; another holding up a crying baby; laughter from a huge cardboard box covered in plastic, and loud snoring from a wigwam. There was a little snow on the ground but at least the rear kitchens of some restaurants were blowing hot air into the alleyway, inadvertently providing some heat for the homeless.

I was about to give up on my search when the figure of a man emerged from a sturdy military tent. 'Could it be Woody?' I thought. Unfortunately, it wasn't, but an elderly bearded guy who spoke with a broken Australian accent. He invited me into his spotlessly clean candlelit 'home' and offered me coffee, which he boiled over a little gas stove. He wore a black beret, like the ones French artists used to wear, and a green combat jacket. He had soulful, chestnut brown eyes and a weather-beaten complexion. There was a subtle smell of perfume in the tent and behind him was a cabinet filled with books; and across the tent was a clothes line with some T-shirts hanging on it, and on the ground was a double inflatable bed and a pair of dumbbells beside it. He told me he used to be a lay-chaplain in a women's prison in Melbourne, Australia, before emigrating to New York. He said he never met Woody, but he matched the description of a man who would sometimes visit the laneway to sell weed. He said the man would have a coffee with him in the tent and even gave him his address, which he passed on to me. We chatted awhile. We both had a deep interest in science.

As I left his tent, I cycled down another laneway, which curved its way round the corporate strip. I heard footsteps in the distance but couldn't tell if they were behind me or in a different street nearby. Then a van drove quickly by and sped up the lane. I turned a corner and decided to drop in on where the man who could be Woody lived. It was a third-floor apartment in the middle of the laneway. I could see a TV flickering through a window, but the main door was locked, so I picked up a small stone and threw it up at the window. A young man opened the door and looked over at me. I explained that I wanted to go up and see my friend, and the man kindly let me in. Arriving at the landing, I knocked on his door a few times but there was no answer; as I was walking away, the door opened. A bearded man in a dressing gowan wearing a baseball hat and spectacles without the lenses, stood motionless and stared at me.

I said, "Woody, is that you?" He never answered. He walked back into the room and stood staring out the window. I followed him into his flat, which was very warm and smelt of burnt grass and fried meat. I remember saying his name again, but he wouldn't turn around. Then he said, "You can't talk to strangers anymore; there's no continuum. There . . . is . . . no . . . continuum." Once again, I said, "Woody . . . It's me, Tom; don't you remember me?" But he just stood there staring down at the street as the rain began to fall. His last words were, "You talk to people here, but they just don't answer you." It was then that I felt a little uneasy; it was like talking to a stranger. Maybe he's gone mad, I thought. Maybe we're all mad? Anyhow, I left his apartment without saying 'goodbye' and continued cycling home. I was never quite sure if he was Woody or someone else living there.

Some three months later, I went back to visit the old man, but I was told by a fellow camper that he died in his sleep on New Year's Day. He said the old man's tent is kept clean and remains as a kind of shrine to those he helped. He said the old man was a bit too friendly with attractive homeless women in the lane who he would give spiritual advice to, and he added, "perhaps a bit more, if you know what I mean." He gave me the address and headstone location of the graveyard the old man was buried in, and, on New Year's Day, I placed flowers on his little headstone.

I'm so glad I escaped a life on the streets. It's been raining all day but at least I'm warm and dry, despite my broken leg. Things could be worse, that's for sure.

Eulogy for Roderic

I was a close buddy of Roderic throughout my college years, but he de-friended me when I told him I was no longer a liberal. He said I betrayed him and all he stood for. But what he and I stood for when we were friends eventually drove me crazy. We ended up parting and going our separate ways.

A few years later, he went missing. None of his friends, nor his children and wife who left him, knew where he was or if he were dead or alive. It came as a big surprise to me a few years ago when I got the news that Roderic died suddenly. I felt a bit guilty that I wasn't upset by the news. It was during the Covid Lockdowns in winter, but some city bars were open, while most of the churches were closed. In the odd church that was open, the priest gave Communion dressed in a space suit, while holding the Host with surgical gloves.

Some guy called Tony, who claimed to be Roderic's close friend, broke the news about Roderic, when he texted me and said he had arranged a eulogy for his deceased buddy in a vacant, old music hall near The Loop in St Louis, close to Washington University. He also texted "all Black Lives Matters comrades of Roderic, and his friends are welcome to attend the eulogy". I remember thinking, what a clever move, as this will keep the cops from raiding the hall during Lockdowns.

That night, I arrived at the dimly-lit hall at 7.30pm, five minutes before it began. At least sitting in the back row, I'd be first out of the hall when the eulogy ended. There must have been about 60 people in the hall and in front of the stage was a bucket with a large fluorescent poster over it with the words: PLEASE DONATE KINDLY FOR A HEADSTONE FOR RODERIC. The bucket was half full of $20 and $50 bills, as well as some jewelry. I threw fifty bucks into it. On the stage was a wicker coffin on a supermarket shopping trolley, beside which stood a podium with a fluorescent sign stating: SEE BUCKET BELOW STAGE FOR DONATIONS FOR RODERIC. Beside the coffin was a bicycle leaning on a table, and on top of the table there was a small collection of Roderic's memorabilia.

When Tony entered the stage, he was dressed in a dark hoodie, wearing a baseball cap, face mask and tinted glasses, while holding an iPhone in his hand. He stood beside the coffin and, with his phone, took a selfie with the coffin in the background. He then stood behind the podium and yawned loudly, while fiddling with some papers. He started to deliver the eulogy in a muffled tone and never removed his cap or mask throughout the entire speech. I thought it disrespectful that he didn't remove his cap, but the congregation, all wearing face masks except me, didn't seem to mind, applauding him during his opening sentence. After yawning, he said: "We meet here today to remember our good friend, Roderic. Roderic was a maverick lecturer in IT studies, and a fine activist for tyrannical minority causes in faraway lands. There wasn't a cause a thousand miles away that he didn't engage in. For Roderic, the farther away, the better. He was also a man of deep faith in Mother Earth. It was at his local bookstore that he first encountered the book, *Making Love to Gaia, Not Raping Her*; a masterpiece by Sir Jamesy Lovestruck; and Roderic committed his whole life to worshiping the Earth and hating the human parasites destroying it, especially white, straight men.

Throughout his life, Roderic held onto his faith with great gusto; and in times of sorrow or joy, he always turned to Lovestruck's work for solace. Roderic believed he was a good father, and, to repeat, a true friend to dark-skinned strangers in faraway lands while his own family starved. In fact, he blindly, and unwittingly, filled the bank accounts of many NGO, CEOs living in sub-Saharan Africa, showing that 'telescopic philanthropy' was not just a vanity project for him to brag about, but a way of unwittingly funding charity bosses in distant lands. As for hobbies, he loved cycling, tweeting toxic abuse to based white males, and vegan cuisine. He was also chairperson of the local Vegan Society and a dedicated campaigner for 'Save the Whales' and other amphibian creatures. And when one of these great Orcas rolled ashore dead with a discarded face mask stuck in his blowhole, Roderic would be the first on the sandy beach with teddy bear and lighted candle in hand.

Despite having a breezy outlook on life, Roderic was miserable, but he kept busy by being an active member of many environmental groups. However, his unwavering faith in Giai made zero impact on our community, and some of us, but not me, might be indifferent for the time we spent together. At the end of the day, we are all automatons ruining the planet. And here (pointing to the coffin) lies the rearrangement of atoms of a grown-up worm in a wicker basket. To be more precise, nothing more than decayed matter in the form of electromagnetic radiation. With great regret, I can't even say 'may he rest in peace', as he'll soon be resting in tiny pieces when the larvae feast upon his rotten carcass in the coming weeks; it'll be the mother of all free lunches for those tiny critters. We humans may be ordered to 'Eat Zee Bugs' but zee bugs will eventually eat all of us.

The saddest part of this eulogy is the fact that Roderic's children ran off and became nuns and priests. Some might call this Hegel's 'cunning of reason', but I call it 'the treason of running'. And before his youngest son ran away, he came out of the closet and told his parents he was straight and wanted to convert to Catholicism. This made Roderic and his wife break down and cry. It happened while the couple were putting up their Ukrainian decorations while celebrating the first round of Covid lockdowns. Roderic said the news left a bad taste in his mouth. He said it was worse than being French-kissed by his grandmother. They knew the stigma and shame of having a straight Catholic son, and it could result in losing all their friends. And as they were both in an open relationship and had many swinger partners, they risked destroying the cheap thrills at weekends. It made me wonder: Where did Roderic go wrong in rearing such dumbos? I guess, some things we'll never know.

At this point, I'd like to show you a few special things in Roderic's life that brought him great joy. (Pointing to the photo) In his hero, Saint Nelson Mandella, we see how justice, freedom and peace now hovers over the great land of South Africa, as tens of thousands of white farmers are being corrected for being racist; and with the globe, we see Roderic's love of the planet and his quest for zero carbon emissions, even though the Earth will eventually be incinerated by the sun in five billion years' time when it becomes a red giant. Roderic cared so much for the planet, he even bought an electric car that had to be charged with fossil fuels; a car that has tens of thousands of young African children forced down narrow, manmade holes in in search of lithium for the car batteries. Then we have his beloved bicycle, which he slept with before getting married. And look at this wonderful photo of Roderic's hero, John Lennon, who sung 'Imagine', a New World Order song that wants to take away all your property and force you to live in a world without countries. And to think that Lennon once said The Beatles were a myth and the biggest bastards on Earth. Ah... a witty man of great humour. He was the glue that kept his generation tightly knit together during the Sexual Revolution. Without The Beatles, we'd probably be STD-free and living in the bosom of families in timber farms surrounded by lakes, forests, mountains, and fresh foods. Indeed, women would be stuck like glue to their houses, baking cookies for the kids instead of being childless, Girl Friday slaves for their fat-cat white male CEOs and stuck to their desks all day and night. Without the Sexual Revolution and Feminism, think of all the millions of women who could've been deprived of going home alone after work and sipping a glass of wine, stroking their cats, while relaxing back and being glued to *Sex and the City*.

Speaking of glue, here we have the super-glue that Roderic used to stick his hand on oil paintings in his local art galleries which he rode to on the oil-based saddle of his beloved bicycle. And here's Roderic's favourite album by Cold Players, the greatest band of all time; and his faithful pooch's lead, with fond memories of long walks by the canal with his dachshund dog, Darwin. Lastly, we have his face mask, which he wore 24/7 throughout the entire pandemic and beyond. The mask also made it possible for him to verbally abuse anti-maskers on the street, as they couldn't see his whole face while filming him. Unfortunately, it was the mask that killed him at the ripe young age of 48, as he broke a red light while shouting at a maskless old lady as she crossed the road. The driver that killed Roderic, did a hit and run. I was the only one of his friends to know about this, as he had left his family a few years ago and went into hiding, almost becoming a recluse.

On a personal level, I'd like to recall one of my favourite memories of Roderic. Many years ago, he was asked to lend a helping hand to migrating toads and frogs who were on their way to their habitual breeding grounds in a rural swampland next to a roadway. The aim to help the frogs migrate was to block a fork in a road that led to the country's biggest old folks' home for sick and dying clergy; a road used by vehicles that brought medical supplies, especially painkillers, to that nuisance nursing home. For Roderic, this home was on the frogs' turf, and as the small creatures were difficult to see, trucks or cars could easily squash them as they made their way across the road on their weekly pilgrimage to the amphibian orgy pond across the roadway. I can see Roderic now in my memory, with a team of Lycra-dressed cyclists, like an army of ants, arm-in-arm, as they blocked the road. On day 10 of the protest, you could hear the distance screams of some old clerics, as the regular delivery of painkilling drugs were blocked by the protesters. When the home eventually closed and the last scream and cries could be heard, Roderic was awarded the Toad Patrol Hero of the Year. As for the old folks' home: That was turned into a sanctuary for stray cats.

In conclusion, I'd like to recite a short poem by Lorissa Z Gluckston, who some years ago won the Nobel Prize for Literature, after winning the Pulitzer Prize for her best-selling book, *Castrate All White Straight Men*. She was Roderic's favourite poet. The poem I'll recite is called 'Tadpoles in My Urine'."

As he cleared his throat, he began to recite the poem:

"I dreamt there were tadpoles in my urine
While frogs hopped all over my bed
And my cats ran for cover in the hallway
Then I awoke and here's what I said:
'Listen to me now, you pack of fat smelly cats
Couldn't catch a frog, you useless puddy tats!'
After much wine, I sat alone feeling less uptight
As I journeyed into the long lonely dark night
It's sad, really: all my life, dying my hair pink
Trying hard to repel men and avoid kitchen sink
No smelly diapers or crying babies to feed
Just a few bottles of wine and packet of weed
Listen to me world, as I sink on the couch

And order a takeaway from Fu Lee's Welcome House
But before I tuck into my Chinese chow mein
I need a man like a frog needs a long wooden cane."

"Such a lovely poem. May Gaia have mercy on Roderic's soul. Thank you, my friends, for paying respect for our deceased friend tonight. Tomorrow, I'll text you with burial arrangements. You may depart now as the hall has to be closed in five minutes."

After a loud yawn, Tony quickly picked up the bucket and went backstage. I must have been the first to walk out of the hall, as I did not want to talk to anyone when the eulogy ended. I walked home through the side streets, and headed for a quiet bar called Skynyrd's, a half-mile from the hall, where patriot types hang out. I often come here as the customers dislike liberals, except for the odd eccentric camp man, resembling an old Edward G Robinson wearing a black beret, who sits alone at the end of the bar with his legs crossed, with a glass of Champagne, while filing his nails. This guy never talks to anyone, but the customers love him.

As I sat at the bar sipping on a beer while watching a round of boxing on TV, Roderic entered the premises and sat down near to me. He wore a backpack with stuff rattling inside as he took it off. "Is this a ghost?" I thought. I could feel my heart pounding rapidly as I said to him,

"Roderic, you're supposed to be dead." He looked at me and smiled and said, "It's true that the old Roderic is dead, but the new Roderic has been red-pilled and no longer believes in all that Green Gaia crap anymore." I told him about the eulogy in the hall and convinced him I wasn't lying by making up some crazy story about him being dead. He told me about going into hiding and becoming a recluse, but he seemed genuinely interested in my eulogy allegation. For some strange reason, he found it funny and was chuckling a lot.

We quickly left the bar and got a taxi that took us to the hall to confront the conman with his bucket of stolen cash. When we got there, the door was locked and the lights turned off. We looked at each other and both of us broke into hysterical laughter. We then hugged each other and Roderic took a selfie of us, with the building in the background. And just as we were about to part, Roderic yawned before making a B-line into an alleyway. I walked home as it started to rain, but with a heavy heart and a bad feeling in my soul. Something didn't seem right. The next day on the news there was a story about a man being mugged near the Loop. He was currently in a coma in hospital and his name was Roderic. "Could it be?" I wondered.

Lift to the Twelfth Floor

It was 10 minutes to midnight when I got the call from my workmate, Ralph. He said, "Meet me at 15 minutes after midnight on the Twelfth Floor, I have something very important to tell you. Believe me, it's urgent." Twelfth Floor was six floors above our office on a building near Wall Street, NYC. At the time I got the call, I was in a bar with some friends talking about the potential dangers of Artificial Intelligence. I worked in finance, but my buddies worked in BigTech. We would sometimes play pool or chat-up pretty girls at the bar.

But on that creepy night, I entered the lift and pressed button number 12. On its way up, the lift stopped at the Tenth Floor. As the doors slowly opened, my old friend Dave, who died of brain cancer a few years ago, stepped into the lift. It was then I knew I was lucid-dreaming: a dream where I'm aware I'm dreaming. A dream that feels unchangingly physical. This happens to me a lot and it is deeply disturbing as it's quite hard to wake up from such a dream, which is almost like being in an awakened state.

The fantom of Dave smiled at me as I ran out of the lift and took to the stairs, my curiosity getting the better of me regarding what Ralph had to say, even it was in a lucid dream. On meeting him on the Twelfth Floor, he told me that I was a figment of his imagination, as were all my work colleagues, who were fantoms, while the external world was a visual eternal matrix with no beginning or end on an eternal loop, from spiritual Big Bang to Big Crunch *ad infinitum*. I thought to myself that such a concept of cyclical patterns, but lacking eternity, has its origins in some Eastern philosophies; also, in *The Gay Science*, Nietzsche wrote about something similar but with eternal recurrence of all events that would mark the ultimate affirmation of life. Nietzsche (or a figment of my imagination) wrote: "What, if some day or night a demon were to steal after you into your loneliest loneliness and say to you: 'This life as you now live it and have lived it, you will have to live once more and innumerable times more; and there will be nothing new in it, but every pain and every joy and every thought and sigh and everything unutterably small or great in your life will have to return to you, all in the same succession and sequence'."

Surely such a concept is crazy? Could my existence be like God but without being all powerful, hence, having limited power? Such an existence would not need a cause nor explanation. If true, I was/am always a Brute Meaningless Fact living out each moment repeatedly on a loop *ad infinitum*, and the odd curious moments of *deja vu* that I sometimes experience, hinted at that; a solipsistic matrix, if you will. This panicked me and I did the usual thing I always do to wake up from the dream: Tapping my heels together.

Coincidently, isn't this what 'Dorothy' did to wake herself up from a lucid dream in the story *The Wizard of Oz*? When I awoke, I was lying in bed alone. I got up to go to the bathroom and prayed that I was not stuck in a lucid-dream type world or subjected to a 'Groundhog Day' situation. In the end, I thought, it all comes down to what is true. How do we know to be true with 100% certainty that the 'other' person has thoughts in his or her head? It seems Truth is the most important question in philosophy. In John 18:37-38, when Jesus stood before Pilate, Pilate said to Him, "So You are a king?" Jesus answered, "You say correctly that I am a king. For this I have been born, and for this I have come into the world, to testify to the truth. Everyone who is of the truth hears My voice." Pilate said to Him, "What is truth?" then he quickly left the room (John 18: 37-38).

When I slowly left the bathroom, I got back into bed and fell asleep. The next morning when I awoke, Ralph called me on the phone. He said: "I can't make it to work today, I'm quite hung-over. I'll see you tomorrow." When he hung up, I could hear him repeat his message again, in a radio-type voiceover. Could it be the lead filling in my tooth that caused this? Or was it a glitch in the matrix?